A Pineville

Autumn Wedding

Book 13

Anne Fons

Scripture taken from the New King James Version®. Copyright © 1982 by Thomas Nelson. Used by permission. All rights reserved.

Cover designed by Valdas Miskinis

This book is a work of fiction. Names, characters, places, and incidents are either products of the author's imagination or are used fictitiously. Any resemblance to actual persons, living or dead, events, or specific locales is entirely coincidental.

Printed in the United States of America

First Printing: September 2022
Anne Fons Readers Group

ISBN: 13-979-8-3549798-4-4

Also by Anne Fons

-FICTION-

Acknowledgements

Writing mentor, best-selling author, and friend,
Winter Travers

Cover designer,
Valdas Miskinis

Advanced Readers, fantastic support system,
and great friends who are always there for me,
Jennie Amato, Rachel Auberger, Tina Carlson,
Sharon Hartlaub, & Shari Huppert.
(Any errors remaining are mine.)

My family, friends, readers,
& God.

Dedication

To Sarah,
our very own
autumn bride

Chapter One

It was cool enough to know fall was coming, but that beautiful, late-summer, Sunday afternoon, still had a hint of warmth. A simple sweater or sweatshirt were all that were required to feel comfortable for sitting outside for the entire afternoon.

Elizabeth snuggled under Rick's arm and spread out across the porch swing at Yarkton House. "I know for sure I want that section we discussed from First Corninthians," she said.

"Is that one from Chapter 13?" asked Rick.

"Yes, I thought it might be nice to have verses four through the beginning of eight early on in the service," said Elizabeth.

Rick looked down at her face, which was still looking in the Bible. "Sweetheart," he said, "I know the message of Chapter 13, but I don't have it all memorized. Which particular part is that?"

"It starts with, 'Love suffers long *and* is kind; love does not envy;'" said Elizabeth. "It goes through the beginning of verse 8 where it says, 'Love never fails.'" She handed him her Bible. "See? It's this section right over here." She pointed to it as she handed him the Book.

Rick read the entire passage that Elizabeth had marked. "I like it. I know it's used for a lot of weddings. I think I've heard it at most of them. Maybe that's because it's so on-point with how a marriage should be."

He started to hand the Bible back to Elizabeth.

"While you're in that part," said Elizabeth, "take a look at verse 15 in that same chapter. I thought it would be nice at the closing of the service."

Rick read aloud. "'And now abide faith, hope, love, these three; but the greatest of these three *is* love.' I like that, too."

"Good," said Elizabeth. "We now have the first and last readings selected."

"Anything else you want me to read while I have this in my hands?" asked Rick.

"Not in First Corinthians, at least not right now," said Elizabeth. "I kind of know which ones I want, but I haven't figured out where they should all go."

"You will," said Rick, "and it will be perfect."

"I was beginning to worry about this," said Elizabeth. "I felt guilty that selecting these readings wasn't the first thing I planned for the wedding itself."

"I don't think you should feel guilty about that," said Rick. "I know you've studied the Bible over the years, but without that list of suggested verses Pastor Plain gave you when we met with him, I don't think you would have found, or thought of, some of these. You've gone through his list, your own, as well as other people's suggestions. Granted, some of those overlap. Look at it this way, Bets; you're not just getting this done. You're getting it done right." He handed the Bible back to her.

"Don't you think almost everyone does it this way? Unless, of course, they really are Biblical scholars or had things picked out since their teenage years," said Elizabeth. "I mean, it's such a special thing."

"That's true," said Rick, "but that doesn't mean people necessarily do it that way. I'm guessing a lot of people either picked the first one they saw on the list or asked the pastor to pick something out for them."

"I guess having Pastor Plain pick them would have been all right with me, too," said Elizabeth, "but every time I see a verse that sounds like something I want for you and me, or that shows something we've been through together, I feel it's something I want in our ceremony."

"Then, that's what's right for us," said Rick.

Elizabeth clutched the Bible to her chest, closed her eyes, and took a deep breath of what still remained of the summer air. "Isn't this an amazing day?" she asked.

Rick stroked her hair and marveled at the beautiful young woman who would soon be his wife. "It is for me."

Chapter Two

Sunday evenings at the Don and Jeannie Anderson home were always full of family, catching up, and food. For as many years as most of them could remember, every available family member would gather at their home around five in the afternoon until after dessert was served and the dishes washed. There was no need for discussion. It was the same every week.

"Jeannie," said Myrtle, "I wish you would let me help you more. You do so much of this work every week, plus you hold down a full-time job running the diner. I'm retired. I have plenty of time to do some of this."

"Myrtle," said Jeannie, "you stay late every week and help me clean up after the crowd. That's a tremendous help to me."

"What are a little dishes and vacuuming?" asked Myrtle. "That's nothing compared to all you do."

"And mopping, and dusting…" said Jeannie.

"Myrt, we've got pret' near a dozen-and-a-half people in this house on a full Sunday," said Deke. "Even I know that's more than 'a little bit of dishes.'"

"Oh, nonsense, Deke," said Myrt, "Jeannie and I don't do those alone. Frankly, there's usually three people at the sink and another two loading up the dishwasher. I have to say, Jeannie, you certainly raised your children to help where it's needed."

"Thank you," said Jeannie, "I'm blessed."

"That's because I'm one of your sons," said Michael as he kissed his mom on the cheek as he passed by. "Face it, Ma," he called over his shoulder, "you know I'm your favorite."

Jeannie smiled as she looked back from her youngest son. "I have three sons," she said, "and two daughters. Plus, two wonderful daughters-in-law."

The six-year-old looked up from playing blocks with three toddlers. "Aren't we your favorites, too, Grandma?" asked Joseph's son, Charlie.

"Absolutely!" said Jeannie. "I have so many favorite people in my life. God has given me so many blessings!"

One of the toddlers tumbled backwards from his sitting position on the living room floor. He began to cry.

Instinctively, his mother picked him up and cuddled him. "It's ok, Jackson," Stephanie said. "You're fine."

She turned her attention back to the family conversation as Jackson squirmed to get back on the floor with his siblings and his cousin.

"Speaking of God," said Joseph's wife, "how did your Bible verse search go today, Elizabeth?"

"It was wonderful," said Elizabeth. "Rick picked one that he knows he wants. We picked a couple we both really like, and the rest, he is leaving up to me."

"How many readings are you going to have?" asked her younger sister, Angela.

"I haven't come up with an exact number," said Elizabeth, "but things are coming together."

"It's a good thing," said her Aunt Bonnie. "That wedding is only a few weeks from now."

"I know," said Elizabeth. "It seems like it's coming up really fast, but at the same time, it seems like it's been forever."

"One look at your relationship over the years should explain that to you," said Joseph.

"You're not going to start on that again, are you?" asked Elizabeth.

"Joseph," cautioned his father, Don.

"No," said Joseph. "I'm only saying the answers for why you feel that way are evident. No one needs to wrack their brain to figure it out."

"You're a 'deer,' you know that?" said Elizabeth.

"Well, thank you," said Joseph.

"Yes, don't get too caught up in the compliment," said Elizabeth. "I was referring to those big bucks that could gore you with their antlers to make their point."

"All right," said Joseph. "I'll take that to mean I'm a force to be reckoned with."

Stephanie raised her eyes to the ceiling. She loved her husband with every ounce of her being but knew that he could be a bit particular when it came to any of his family members and what he perceived as their mistakes.

"Whatever you want to believe, Brother 'Deer,'" said Elizabeth.

"What's on the menu tonight, Ma?" asked Michael as he came back into the living room.

"You already peeked. So, you tell me," said Jeannie.

Michael feigned innocence. "Me??"

"Yes, you," said Jeannie.

"Seriously," said Michael, "how did you know that?"

"You've been doing it since you were a kid," said his Uncle Deke. "We could all have told you that."

"Aw, and here I thought I was so surreptitious," said Michael.

"Not hardly," said Elizabeth.

"Ok," said Michael, "it's barbecue sandwiches, potato salad, cucumber salad, a fruit platter, and cheesecake – but it doesn't look like yours, Aunt Bonnie."

"Maybe you should get him into the sheriff's department, Joseph," said Bonnie. "I didn't bake it. Myrtle did."

"Didn't it look all right to you, Michael?" asked Myrtle. "I know I'm not a professional baker like your Aunt Bonnie, but my cheesecake is usually well-received."

Myrtle's tendency to be terse was beginning to show. Every person in the room listened intently for Michael's reply.

"Well, I think I had better to go back in the kitchen and try a piece right now," said Michael.

Michael's attempt at escape from his hurting of Myrtle's feelings was short-lived.

"Now, you listen here," said Deke. "I've eaten my Myrtle's cheesecake once or twice, and it's delicious. Every bit as tasty as your aunt's. They're different types of recipes, and there's no reason why we can't enjoy both in this family."

Michael looked stunned, but quickly recovered. "That's what I'm saying, Uncle Deke! Deliciousness all around!"

"You're not touching that cheesecake until after dinner, Michael," said Jeannie. "Your Aunt Myrtle gets to serve that."

It was odd for the family to hear Uncle Deke's new wife referred to as 'Aunt Myrtle.' All the years they had known her, which was all of their lives, she was, "Mrs. Hodges." It was only after Deke married Myrtle in June that they needed to change what they called her. Deke didn't want his wife being referred to as 'Mrs. Hodges' anymore. He understood why people slipped into that, as that's what she had been called for the past forty years. However, he had waited a long time to get married and really wanted the honor of having his wife referred to as 'Mrs. Anderson,' or in the case of family, 'Aunt Myrtle.'

"In that case," said Michael, "I had better confess. I snuck a little taste while I was in the kitchen."

"You did what?" asked Myrtle.

"Yeah, I did," said Michael, "and it's delicious!"

"Well," said Myrtle, "I didn't expect people to sample it before it was served, but I'm glad you like it."

"You're going to make this again, aren't you, *Aunt* Myrtle?" said Michael. He gave her a sly grin that conveyed he knew he was working on her heartstrings.

"Well," said Myrtle, "if you like it, and if Bonnie is ok with me doing this from time-to-time."

"I'm fine," said Bonnie. "By the way, I snuck a sample of it, too."

"What?" said Myrtle. "Really? How many little holes am I going to find in that cake?"

"I covered mine up," said Michael.

"I did, too," said Bonnie.

"I guess I should be flattered that you like it," said Myrtle. "I'm just not used to people eating before being served."

"Well, anytime you want to pick up a part-time job, the bakery would be happy to have you," Bonnie said. "That cheesecake is really good!"

"First-rate," said Deke.

"I'm not looking for a part-time job," said Myrtle. "However, if you're ever in a bind, just give me a call. I'd be happy to help in a pinch."

"Would you really?" asked Bonnie.

"Yes," said Myrtle. "Deke works so many hours around the campground. When he's gone, I sometimes look for things to do."

"Careful," said Deke.

"Why?" asked Myrtle.

"I know this bunch. They'll have something for you to do darn near every day," Deke said.

"Gamma, Gamma, Gamma, Gamma, Gamma," said Margaret as she toddled over to Myrtle.

Myrtle picked up the little girl and put her on her lap. "Jeannie," she said, "I hope you don't mind that she calls me Grandma, too. I feel like I'm imposing myself or stepping over boundaries I shouldn't cross."

"Nonsense," said Jeannie. "You have watched over Julia as much as we have since she arrived here in Pineville, and you babysit for Little Margaret as much or more than we do. If it wouldn't have been for you retiring from the secretarial position at the church, Julia may never have come here – or met our Lucas. If she and Lucas hadn't have gotten married, well, then there would be no Little Margaret in our family. So, it all works out."

"That doesn't give me 'grandma' rights," said Myrtle.

"Maybe not," said Lucas. He gave his wife a side hug. "But, Julia and I do. You and Mom have been as close to mother figures as Julia has had in a quite some time. The way you dote on Little

Margaret is as grandmotherly as it gets."

"I don't 'dote,'" Myrtle said in a firm tone as she hugged Margaret and told her, in a very sweet tone, what a little angel she was.

"I see that," said Don.

"She loves being with you," said Julia.

"See what I mean?" said Deke. "Babysitting, the bakery, next thing you know, Jeannie will be asking you to work at the diner."

"What's family for if they can't be called on to help?" said Myrtle. "I had good in-laws with Arthur's family, but they were not at all like this. Plus, when we moved back to Pineville, we only saw them a handful of times each year. I'm delighted to be included."

"Auntie Myrtle?" said Michael.

"*Auntie*?" said Joseph. "Seriously? Did you go back to being twelve?"

"I was just thinking about some of those beautiful lunches Uncle Deke raves about when he comes back from the house after lunch," said Michael. "Apparently, Aunt Myrtle's lunches compare to what we eat for supper."

"So?" said Joseph.

"So, I eat, too," said Michael. "Mom works in the middle of the day. I have to come back here and make myself a sandwich or something."

"You poor guy," said Joseph. "You're in your twenties, and you have to make your own sandwich? Aw."

"I also seem to recall that you have spent many of those lunch hours at the diner where your father makes your meal for you," said Jeannie.

"Shhh," said Michael, "how can I get Aunt Myrtle to feel sorry for me and invite me to lunch if you guys blow my poor, beleaguered, campground worker story?"

"Oh, brother," said Stephanie.

"You're always welcome, Michael," said Myrtle.

"Now, just wait a dad-blamed minute," said Deke. "I like to spend some private time with my sweetie. You ain't going to be coming over every day."

"Once a week, Uncle Deke?" asked Michael.

"Kids," said Deke.

"It's fine, Deke," said Myrtle. "It will be nice to have company over. Once a week sounds nice. Doesn't it, Dear?"

"I told you, didn't I?" said Deke.

"Told me what?" asked Myrtle.

"I told you if you start offering to help, you're going to get more than you bargained for," said Deke.

"Gamma, Gamma, Gamma," said Margaret as she buried her head in the older woman's neck.

"I think I'll be okay," said Myrtle.

"You sure have had a lot of changes in your life over the past few months, Myrtle," said Jeannie. "Between the wedding on such short notice, and then, Stephanie's parents wanting to buy your house."

Myrtle buried her face in her hands for a moment. "Oh, yes, the house."

"As you know, they had been looking for a small house in the Pineville downtown area since around the time Joseph and I got married," said Stephanie. "I'm surprised Mom waited for you to cut the cake at your reception before she brought it up to you."

"Stephanie's mother can be a bit, shall we say, spontaneous," said Joseph.

"A little more than necessary, is what I'd say," said Deke. He looked across the living room to Joseph's wife, "Sorry if I hurt your feelings, Stephanie."

Stephanie shook her head no. "Just let me know if she gets on your nerves," she said. "She has always said what's on her mind – whenever she thinks it. It just popped out of her mouth during your reception. I thought my dad was going to crawl in a hole."

"Your dad's a good egg," said Deke.

"Yes, he is," said Stephanie. "Mom is sweet, too. She just has a problem with waiting for a more opportune time to say things."

"The house wasn't going to go anywhere," said Deke. "She could have waited until we figured out where we were going to live first."

"True, but she didn't want the house to slip away from them for lack of saying something," said Stephanie. "She just had a feeling it was the way God wanted their new home out here to come to be. You know, serendipity."

"They had been looking for a Pineville house for so long," said Jeannie. "It seemed that everything that came on the market was either too big, too far out of town, had too many needed repairs, or was bought before they could get here to look at it."

"Yet, she wanted to buy Myrtle's place without even seeing it first," said Bonnie. "I was surprised."

Stephanie shrugged her shoulders. "That's my mom."

"When's their move-in day?" asked Bonnie.

"Soon," said Deke. "Johnny doesn't want to move once the snow starts falling, and I can't blame him for that."

"Barbara and I are discussing whose furniture will look best in the various rooms," said Myrtle. "They're getting a moving truck later in the week, and she's going to start putting in the pieces she wants from the Milwaukee house. Whatever is left after your mom sets the house up the way she wants it, Stephanie, is going either to a rummage sale or to charity."

"They're doing this before my wedding?" asked Elizabeth.

"Yep," said Deke. "It makes no fool sense to me, except for the 'no snow' part. There shouldn't be snow the end of October, either. I think Johnny would have been okay with waiting another few weeks, but Barbara wouldn't hear of it. Kept saying she needed to have a place here before your wedding, Elizabeth, so that if anyone needed a place for the little ones later in the evening, you could drop them off by her."

Jeannie laughed. "That is certainly sweet of her, but I'm not sure she knows exactly what she's in for if Julia and Stephanie take her up on her offer. Five kids, three of them only one-year-olds? That's a lot of work."

"My dad knows better than to say anything at all to her about overload when it comes to those grandkids," said Stephanie.

"How did the subject of furniture come up?" asked Bonnie.

"She realized her dining room set didn't stand a chance of fitting in Myrtle's kitchen once they went over there," said Stephanie.

"Myrt and Barbara talk almost every day," said Deke.

"Really?" asked Elizabeth.

"Yep," said Deke. "Johnny and I get on the phone when the two wives tell us we have to. Otherwise, we let the women work it out."

"Can you just picture those two men discussing kitchen curtains and night tables?" asked Myrtle.

"My brother would have gone crazy on the first phone call," said Don.

"Are you and Rick still planning on dividing time between your two places, Elizabeth?" asked Michael.

"We almost have to right now," said Elizabeth. "I only have my bedroom and my bathroom for privacy at Yarkton House. Yet, I need to be around, particularly on the weekends for my guests."

"What about Rick's place?" asked Angela. "That's a full apartment."

"And it's right above the restaurant," said Michael. "It couldn't be more convenient for him."

"That does work out better in some ways," said Elizabeth. "We have our own living room and kitchen there, and definitely more privacy than at the bed and breakfast."

"Then why not move there?" asked Angela.

"I feel I would have to give Bridget a sizable raise to handle more of the guest situations, which we really can't afford to do that at this point," said Elizabeth. "Plus, I like being there. The clinic is right downstairs for any veterinary emergencies, and there's the B&B. It's a lot of responsibility, and it's all centered at Yarkton House."

"How long are you going to keep that up?" asked Jeannie. "You know how stressed you were last winter and spring when you tried to take on too much."

Elizabeth held up her hand. "I remember," she said. "Rick

and I do have a plan, but we have to talk to a couple of people before I can say for sure what we want to do."

"I'm almost afraid to ask this question," said Deke, "but who would those 'people' be?"

Elizabeth walked over and stood close to her uncle. She linked her arm through his and said, "Well, now that you mention it, Uncle Deke…"

The rest of the family laughed as Elizabeth began to lay out her and her fiancé's plans for the newest set of renovations at Yarkton House.

Chapter Three

"**S**o, you sprang it on him just like that?" asked Rick as he snapped his fingers. His hair was still damp from his shower, and he cradled his cell phone under his chin as he went about his morning routine in the small kitchen of his apartment over the pizza parlor.

"Well, he did ask," said Elizabeth with a laugh.

"I guess I was right after all," said Rick.

"About what?" asked Elizabeth.

"I told you the right time to ask him would come up," said Rick.

He added some cream to his morning coffee, and his spoon clinked the side of his cup as he stirred it into the strong, dark brew.

"Did you make espresso this morning?" asked Elizabeth.

"No, but it is an Italian roast. Why?" asked Rick. "Also, how did you know I made coffee? You're at your place, and I'm at mine."

"I heard your spoon clink," said Elizabeth.

"Remind me never to say anything under my breath around you," said Rick. "Your hearing would rival a bat's."

Elizabeth let out another soft laugh. "It's not that hard, Rick. You make coffee every morning after your run."

"True," said Rick. "I always make my juice first, though. So, I'm at least somewhat health conscious. Now, if you guess what ingredients went in that juice, I'm definitely going to worry about hidden cameras in this place."

"Ok," said Elizabeth as she closed her eyes and searched her mind, "I am going to say, spinach, carrot and ginger."

"What the heck?" asked Rick. "You missed the green apple, but you had the rest right. How did you do that?"

"I'm psychic this morning," said Elizabeth.

"I almost believe that," said Rick.

"Nah," said Elizabeth, "I saw those ingredients in your refrigerator yesterday when I was over at your place. I didn't see any apples, though."

"That's because I just bought that at the gas station on my way back from my run," said Rick.

"That explains it," said Elizabeth. "I thought I was losing my touch."

"Seriously," said Rick, "you are just like Joseph."

"What?!" said Elizabeth.

It was Rick's turn to laugh. "I meant how you notice things. Joseph does that. Michael does, too. What is it with you Andersons? Are you all wanting to be detectives or something?"

"Not hardly," said Elizabeth. "You couldn't pay me enough to do that job. Seeing people at their worst?" She shuddered. "No, that's not me, although I think the rest of the family, including Angela, could handle it."

"Are you saying you're the wimp of the family?" Rick asked.

"Yes," said Elizabeth. "Definitely. I'll take that title in my particular group."

"You are not a wimp," said Rick. "I was only teasing you. There's no way you could do surgeries on animals or handle some of the circumstances you do if you had no fortitude."

"Thank you," said Elizabeth. "It's different than Joseph's, though. He's not afraid to take on almost anything."

"His form of courage takes on the bad guys and helps keep the rest of us safe," said Rick.

"Rick, I love you," said Elizabeth, "but spaying an animal is not the same as making the world a safer place."

"No," said Rick, "however, you help or save animals every day."

"I'm grateful I can," said Elizabeth.

"And you saved me," said Rick.

"That's sweet," said Elizabeth, "but as much as I would like to believe that I am your one and only everything, I'm also a realist. You would have been just fine without me in your life. Some time or another, someone would have come along that could make you happy."

"I take back what I said," said Rick. "If you still don't know how miserable I felt without you, and how much I need you in my life every day, you're not observant at all."

"Oh, come on, Rick," said Elizabeth. "I know you dated other people when we were apart."

"Yes."

"Are you going to tell me that you never enjoyed yourself, that you were always pining for me?" she asked.

"Sure, I enjoyed myself," said Rick. "It was fine. It was occasionally fun, but it never had the same feeling."

"You're the best boyfriend I could ever wish for," said Elizabeth.

"Hopefully, I will be the best husband, too," said Rick.

"I think you will," said Elizabeth. "I wouldn't marry you if I didn't."

Rick took another sip from his coffee cup. "Well, I'm not sure you talking to your Uncle Deke without me about our housing thoughts qualifies me for being there when you need me."

Elizabeth looked out the front window of her bedroom.

The traffic on Main Street was beginning to pick up a bit. It was the start of what passed for 'rush hour.' In a small town like Pineville, that meant seeing more than one car at a time.

"It was fine, Rick," said Elizabeth. "We all know you work on Sunday nights, and unfortunately, that's when most family conversations take place for us. The family gathering at mom and dad's for supper is kind of a cue for everyone to talk about their weeks and to ask for whatever they want, whether that's advice or help. In our case, I wanted both. So, I asked."

"How did Deke take it?" asked Rick.

"Oh, he put up his usual somewhat-gruff front," said Elizabeth, "but we all know that's not how he really feels."

"Did he have any concerns about making those renovations to the attic?" asked Rick. "That's going to be another huge project for him."

"He's on board," said Elizabeth. "With the size of your apartment, and the fact that Yarkton House is not only my home, but the site of both of my businesses, he knew it would happen sooner rather than later. We just moved it up a year or two from my original plans."

"Well," said Rick, "if you recall, we weren't even dating when you first bought the place. There would have been no rush to get up to that third floor. The higher priorities were to get your clinic running so that you had a place to work, and then getting some of the second-floor bedrooms redone so that you could bring in B & B revenue."

"Uncle Deke has always been there for me," said Elizabeth. "I don't know what I would have done if it weren't for him. I probably couldn't have bought this place. It would have been cost prohibitive to hire a general contractor."

"I wish you wouldn't say that," said Rick.

"About the contractor?" asked Elizabeth.

"No," said Rick, "about you not buying Yarkton House."

"Why?" asked Elizabeth.

"Because it's a reminder of how close we came to never being together," said Rick.

"I believe God would have worked it out some other way," said Elizabeth.

"Maybe," said Rick, "but it makes me a little sick to my stomach just to think about us not being 'us.'"

A couple of school buses went past Elizabeth's window. "The buses are starting to come through," she said.

"Well, we know what that means," said Rick.

"Yes, if it's the start of the school day, it's the start of my workday," said Elizabeth. "I'd better head downstairs. I'm guessing Bridget already has one or two customers in the waiting room."

Chapter Four

It had been a few months since her move, but Myrtle was still getting used to living in Deke's house. The sizes of both their homes were comparable. Neither one of them had large dwellings, both preferring to have only the amount of living space they really needed on a daily basis. The living rooms were large enough to fit a few guests, yet cozy for two people. The bedrooms were of average size, and the bathrooms were made for efficiency not luxury or lounging. All in all, Myrtle felt comfortable in her new surroundings.

However, there were certain things that were different. When she wasn't fully concentrating on being in her new home, she found herself reaching into cupboards for items that weren't there or turning right instead of left to get to the first-floor bathroom.

The area was definitely different. Myrtle had lived near the downtown area of town. She was accustomed to a neighborhood feeling and knowing who her neighbors were. She had a small backyard and a front yard with a few rosebushes. Her lot was typical for a city or town.

Deke's home was set at the northern edge of the family property. It was set off from the campground area to offer a modicum of privacy from the guests who resided or visited during the camping season. When Myrtle looked out her front window of her new house, she didn't see her neighbors getting their mail or newspapers, she saw nature.

Rarely a day went by without Myrtle seeing some sort of

wildlife. Often that came in the form of squirrels, birds, and rabbits. Yet, Myrtle had also seen foxes, opossum, and deer. All in all, when she was being honest with herself, she knew that she would vastly prefer seeing a deer in the trees to her neighbor in his bathrobe.

The occasional camper coming through the trails took a little more getting used to. Myrtle was never a chatty woman and making small talk with them did not come naturally to her. She told herself that this was her husband's land and his livelihood and that she needed to do her best to make everyone feel welcome.

Her 'husband.' Myrtle mulled that little phrase in her mind more than once.

Many years ago, she had been married to Arthur Hodges, and she thought that would be all the days of her life. After he passed away, she spent many years as a single woman, raising her daughter, being a secretary for the Pineville Community Church, and taking part in things such as bake sales, book clubs, and knitting many items to gift or give away. She had found a rhythm to her life, and she was content.

Then, suddenly, Deke came back into her life. Myrtle had thought that part of her life was only to be part of her memories of her youth.

Yet, *'God had other plans.'*

That's how she described her whirlwind courtship back into Deke's arms and starting a completely new phase of her life.

Myrtle sighed as she mused about how many changes there had been for her over the course of only a few months. From being single and planning on being a Mother of the Bride, to *being* the bride, to moving into Deke's home, and now selling the house she had lived in for all those years since she and Arthur moved back to Pineville.

She smiled. She was happy she and Deke found their love for each other once more.

The ringing of the house telephone brought Myrtle back from her musings. She looked at the time on the wall clock and was pretty sure she knew who was on the other end of the line. She sighed.

Myrtle tended to keep her telephone conversations short and to the point with the exception of when she spoke to her daughter, Susan, or a teenage girl named Chloe, whom she had befriended a while ago. However, this call would not be short, and she knew it.

"Hello," she said.

"Hello, Myrtle, Barbara Cannady here," said the woman.

"I thought it might be you," said Myrtle. "You had mentioned calling me when you got back from your hair appointment."

"Oh, my goodness how I needed that haircut! You wouldn't have believed the traffic on the way there, though. Can you believe some fool was driving on a main Milwaukee street with a mattress that wasn't tethered down? A main street! He was just hanging on to one side of it. Well, needless to say, that fell off, and the rest of us had to wait until he retrieved it…"

Myrtle was starting to become accustomed to Stephanie and her mother's strung together sentences. Both mother and daughter could go on for minutes seemingly without taking a breath. She waited for an opening. "Oh, yes, that was a ridiculous thing to do. Well, I'm glad you're home now. Did you want to talk about the house?"

"Yes," said Barbara, "I have a few more questions for you before we come up this weekend. You know, Stephanie and Joseph said they would help. I guess most of the Andersons are coming. Then again, you probably already know that now that you are an Anderson, too."

"Well," said Myrtle, "I heard the family's conversation last Sunday at Don and Jeannie's."

Myrtle knew if she left too long of a gap between her sentences that Barbara would start talking again, so she hurried on. "What would you like to know about the house?"

Myrtle was still on the phone with Barbara when Deke and Michael walked in the door. "Barbara, I need to go. The men are here for lunch, and I'm afraid I still haven't set the table."

"Oh, dear," said Barbara. "I will let you go. Johnny was never able to come home from work for lunch, but Tim and Stephie, they came home all during grade school."

"Yes," said Myrtle, "then you know what it's like to have to scramble fast so they can get back to school or work."

Once more she hurried to get in a sentence, "I'll see you next weekend!"

She hung up the phone and turned to Deke and Michael.

"Stephanie's mother?" asked Deke.

Myrtle shook her head. "Yes. She means well, but she goes on and on about almost everything."

Michael laughed. "I've heard."

"Everybody's heard," said Deke. "I've seen people go the other way when they see her coming. Not because they don't like her, but because she never stops yammering about things."

"Have you talked to her much, Uncle Deke?" asked Michael.

"Not when I can avoid it," said Deke. "I mostly talk to her husband. Johnny gets to the point."

"I'm almost sorry we sold her the house," said Myrtle. "She is driving me crazy with all her questions! Honestly, anything from the furnace to the curtain on the back door. I think I've answered a hundred questions."

"Well," said Deke, "they're moving in next weekend. So, then they'll get settled."

"Do you think she's going to stop calling and asking about every little thing?" asked Myrtle.

Deke chuckled. "Not for a minute."

Michael sniffed the air. "Aunt Myrtle, do I smell meatloaf?"

"Yes, and there's mashed potatoes and green beans to go with it," said Myrtle.

"That's my Myrt," said Deke. "I'll bet she has something for dessert, too, since she knew you were coming."

Myrtle looked at Deke. "Now you went and let the cat out of the bag," she said. "I was going to surprise him with those brownies."

"I'm still surprised," said Michael, "and I'm hungry, too!"

Chapter Five

Elizabeth sneezed as she made her way up the steep, winding stairs to the expansive, dusty attic of the Yarkton House. "Oh, man, the dust up here! I am going to have to start coming up here to clean on a regular basis. I didn't realize this much dust could accumulate in an unused space, especially since I did this when I tackled my spring cleaning."

Rick came up the stairs behind her. "Nobody ever comes up here right now. I don't think you have to worry about doing that until maybe a week or so before we begin remodeling this."

"But, it's a dusty mess," said Elizabeth.

Rick stood next to her and looked all the way around the large area. "Who's going to care for the next few weeks, the spiders?"

Elizabeth shuddered. "I hate spiders, but don't tell my patients with tarantulas that," she said with a smile. "After cleaning so many of them out of the basement, yuck. I thought I was done with the bulk of those eight-legged creatures."

"It was a joke, Bets," said Rick. He took a few steps and peered at one of the corners of the woodwork. "I don't see a single one right now."

"Maybe not," said Elizabeth, "but why do I get the feeling they are going to hold a convention up here once I begin cleaning this out?"

Rick gave her a kiss on the cheek. "If you run into an army of them, give me a call. I'll take over."

"Thank you, Sweetheart," said Elizabeth. She gave him a quick kiss as well.

They both looked all around the space and took some basic measurements.

"Do you think I am overextending myself again?" Elizabeth asked.

Rick looked at her as he retracted the measuring tape. "Are you talking about physically, emotionally, or financially?"

"Well, all of it, I guess," she said, "but mainly in terms of taking on too much work right before our wedding. I don't want to show up exhausted for our ceremony."

"If this is too much right now, you say so," said Rick. "I don't want that, either, and we can certainly make do for a year or so if we have to do so."

"There won't be much privacy for us here," said Elizabeth.

"There's some," said Rick. "At least you have your own little suite with a bedroom and bathroom."

"Yes, and the rest of the house is pretty much communal – except for the clinic, of course," said Elizabeth.

"We can always stay at my place," said Rick. "There we will have a kitchen and a living room to ourselves as well. I thought we worked this out, Bets. We were going to stay at my place Monday-Thursday night and here on the weekends when the B & B is the busiest. Have you changed your mind? Are you thinking that won't work now?"

Elizabeth walked over to one of the trunks in the attic and gently ran her finger over the cover. "No, I still think that's workable for now, but I'm not sure how long I want to bounce between two places, even if they are less than a half-mile apart."

"How much do you have left to do on the wedding plans?" asked Rick.

"Other than matching the Bible verses with the people who will be reading them," said Elizabeth, "I don't have much to do until the week before. Then, I need to switch back to wedding mode. I can't believe how much there is to do at the last minute!"

"So, what you're saying is that we need to start talking about the renovations now if we have a prayer of getting in here before a couple of years roll by," said Rick.

"Not necessarily at this very moment, but soon," said Elizabeth. "Uncle Deke wants to start making some basic plans. He wants to start on it as soon as possible after our wedding."

"That makes sense," said Rick, "the campground is closed then. Aren't he and Myrtle going somewhere, though? I know they talked about heading someplace once the campground was closed for the season. They didn't get much time for just the two of them after the wedding."

"True," said Elizabeth, "but it won't be until after the holidays. Susan convinced them to come to Florida for a month this winter."

"Seriously?" said Rick. "Your uncle never goes anywhere."

"He does if Myrtle says so," said Elizabeth.

Rick shook his head. "Ah. Got it. I keep forgetting the dynamics have changed."

Elizabeth smiled and nodded.

Rick looked around. "Then, how is he going to fit in working on the attic?" he asked.

"Uncle Deke told me that he wants to do a walkthrough before the wedding," said Elizabeth. "He will get all of our ideas, and give us his thoughts, along with a sense for the cost. He will start ordering the materials that take a while to arrive and would like us to make any changes that we want by Thanksgiving. He said we should take the month of December to thoroughly gut the attic and clean. January first, he's starting here. He will get a lot of the basics done before February."

"Ok," said Rick. "What's happening in February?"

"That's when he and Myrtle will be gone," said Elizabeth. "So, obviously, he won't be able to do anything here then. However, his goal is that he will have some things ready for work that you and Michael can do. Heads up, though, he has Michael covering any shoveling and plowing that might need to be done while he's gone."

"So, Michael is unavailable in February, too?" asked Rick.

"To a degree," said Elizabeth. "The plowing isn't a full-time job unless there's a huge snowfall. I think he would be able to help us most days."

"What about all those other odd jobs he takes?" asked Rick.

"You're worrying too much," said Elizabeth. "He did all that before when we did the clinic and the guest rooms. Somehow, he balances it all. As long as he doesn't fall in love, he'll be here."

"Keep him away from gorgeous women until our project is done, ok?" asked Rick.

Elizabeth let out a laugh. "I'll do my best."

Chapter Six

Deke had a legal pad, graph paper, rulers, calculator, and pencils spread out in front of him on the large, wooden, dining room table at Yarkton House.

Rick sat across from him. Although his arsenal of tools was smaller, he had a notebook, pens, and calculator ready.

"I want to thank you for doing this for Bets and me," said Rick. "I know your schedule is busier now that you're married."

"My schedule's not really all that different," said Deke, "but I sure like coming home to a house that's not empty; especially when it's Myrt that greets me when I get there."

"I hear you're heading to Florida this winter," said Rick.

"Yes, Myrt's daughter, Susan, wants her mom to spend some time where it's warmer," said Deke.

"How do you feel about that?" asked Rick.

Deke shrugged. "Makes no never mind to me one way or the other," he said. "I like it here, and I wasn't looking to go anywhere, but I promised Myrtle that we would go whenever Susan wanted us there. Myrt sure misses her."

"I imagine," said Rick.

Elizabeth came into the room with a pitcher of lemonade and some cookies.

Deke put a few of the delicate cherry ones on his platter. "Don't you go telling Myrt I ate these," said Deke. "She says I eat too many sweets."

Elizabeth smiled. "I wouldn't think of it."

Deke took a bite of his cookie before he proceeded. "Now, tell me all about what your thoughts are for this attic."

The three talked at length about ways to make the space both usable and comfortable. Elizabeth offered her dreams that she had envisioned when she first purchased Pineville's grandest home. Rick offered some suggestions on unique ways to make the best use possible of the deep slope in the ceiling, as well as the little nooks and crannies that were tucked within corners and around the chimney. Deke used every architectural skill he had, combined with his years of carpentry and contracting at the campground.

By the end of the evening, Deke used a large, expansive sheet of white paper to do a rough sketch for them of what he thought they wanted to work into the finished project. When he turned it around, and pointed out the different aspects of the plan, Elizabeth was overcome with emotion.

"Oh, wow, Uncle Deke!" she said, "I never thought it would be this incredible!"

"Of course, now, you know sometimes things have to change once we start the work," said Deke. "Things can pop up for which we did not plan."

"I know," said Elizabeth. "I remember from the main floors."

"Are you ready for some basic numbers?" asked Deke.

Elizabeth held her breath.

Rick said, "We need to know. So, now is as good a time as any."

Deke showed them a list of line items, corresponding numbers, and a working total at the bottom.

Elizabeth gasped. "I thought it might come in too high. We can take out some of that, use different windows…"

"Hey," said Rick. He touched her arm. "Bets, you need to take a breath here."

"Rick, it's too expensive," said Elizabeth, "but I'm not giving up yet. I know how to trim things back. I did it before."

He gave her arm a gentle squeeze. "You are forgetting something very important," said Rick.

"What's that?" asked Elizabeth. Though she had said she

wasn't upset about making changes, both Rick and Deke could see some disappointment on her face.

"You're not in this alone anymore," said Rick. "You have me. You have my income. You have my restaurant that we can use as collateral on a loan."

"Stop right now, Rick," said Elizabeth. She turned her face toward him and away from the drawings and the numbers in front of her.

"Why?" asked Rick.

"I can't let you put your restaurant at risk," said Elizabeth. "Your name isn't even on the title of Yarkton House yet."

"First of all," said Rick, "I don't consider this high-risk. We're going to be living in it. If push comes to shove, we can rent it out while living at my place. Plus, we will also have your existing suite to rent once you move from your current bedroom."

Elizabeth looked at him.

"Second," he continued, "whether you put my name on this place or not, I'm still committed to doing this. We are getting married in less than three weeks. Do you honestly think I expect you to pay for everything? This is where I will live, too, remember."

"I know that," said Elizabeth. "If we weren't getting married, this would still be a project for about five years from now."

"Do you want to do something else in the meantime?" asked Rick. "It's not impossible to keep our original arrangement of splitting time between the apartment and here. Of course, that could become a little more challenging if we have a baby. Then again, I could ask my dad to switch apartments with me."

Rick looked over at Deke. "As you know, he's living in the one where I grew up. There are two bedrooms in that one. Dad offered to do that even now for us if we want more space."

"I told you I won't hear of your dad relocating just for us," said Elizabeth. "Especially since we plan on having our own space as soon as we can. It would be hard on him."

"I think you are worried about that more than he is," said Rick. "You know he would move heaven and earth for you.

Sometimes, I think my dad is even happier about this marriage than I am. Then again, I know that's impossible. So, I'm ok."

"Well, I'll tell you what," said Deke, "I will leave these plans and costs with you. Take your time. Figure things out for yourselves. I'm in no hurry, and I don't plan on even starting this until after the wedding."

Once Deke had packed up his things and left, Rick and Elizabeth continued their conversation.

Being a mid-week evening, there weren't many guests in the B & B, and no one else was on the main floor with them. They sat on the couch in the parlor, each sipping an evening cup of herbal tea.

"You look tense," said Rick.

"I guess I am," said Elizabeth.

He put down his cup and moved closer to her. He began to massage her shoulders. "Is this better?"

"Much."

"Can I ask you something without starting another argument?" asked Rick.

"What?" asked Elizabeth. Her shoulders contracted.

"Whoa!" said Rick.

"What's the matter?" asked Elizabeth.

"Just mentioning asking you something put every knot back into your shoulders that I have been trying to work out of them," said Rick.

"I'm sorry," said Elizabeth.

"You don't need to be sorry, Bets," said Rick, "but please, Sweetheart, try to relax a little. I'm not going to take your head off."

"I know that," said Elizabeth. "I guess I'm being childish."

Rick stopped massaging her shoulders. "Huh? I'm not sure I get where that comes from."

"Oh, you know," said Elizabeth, "I am sadder than I thought I would be about the attic coming in higher than we anticipated."

"Ok," said Rick, "but how does that translate into being childish?"

"The princess isn't getting her dream castle," said Elizabeth, "so I'm sitting here pouting about it instead of making the needed adjustments."

She turned to face him. "I don't get it, Rick," she said. "I had to make modifications to the other renovations here, and it never bothered me for more than a brief moment. This time, I'm acting like somebody told me my dog died. I don't understand why I am reacting like this."

He took her face in his hands. "Look, Honey, I don't have all the answers, either, but I think in a strange way, you kind of nailed it."

"How so?" asked Elizabeth.

"You said you weren't getting your castle," said Rick.

"I always thought of Yarkton House as sort of Pineville's answer to a castle," said Elizabeth. "It's big. It's grand. It's beautiful, and I am lucky to have it in any format. I'm a little ashamed of myself."

"You need to stop it," said Rick.

"I know," said Elizabeth. "I truly am sorry for being such a baby about this."

"That's not what I mean," said Rick. "You need to stop beating yourself up for your dreams and your wants in life. We all have things we desire. I can't buy you a castle in Europe, and I can't give you the world on a silver plate, but I can help you with this place."

Elizabeth shook her head no. "I can't let you use the restaurant for it. We'll get by with just the basic structure for now, and we can add other things in later."

"Somewhat," said Rick, "but there are a few things that if we take them out of the build now, they are going to be twice as hard to put them in at a future date, not to mention more expensive."

"So, what can we do without risking your restaurant?" asked Elizabeth.

Rick walked over to the drawings, which were still on the dining room table. He stared at them for a while. "I think most of it."

Chapter Seven

"This dining room table has seen a lot of non-dining activity lately," said Elizabeth. She brought a shoe box full of small envelopes and set it in between her and Rick.

"Are all of those response cards for the wedding?" asked Rick. "If they're all yesses, we're going to have to spill out of the clubhouse and onto the campgrounds."

"I can't help you had to invite every relative down to the third cousins," said Elizabeth. "Are you even going to recognize them all?"

"Nope," said Rick, "but my Zietta Nerva will."

"Your Aunt Nerva certainly thinks she is the family matriarch," said Elizabeth. "She scares the life out of me."

Rick laughed. "You and most other people."

"Lovely," said Elizabeth. "I'm not looking forward to being scrutinized by her, and I have a real sinking feeling she is going to do just that."

"Don't worry," said Rick, "she's putty in my hands."

"Ha!" said Elizabeth. "Your Aunt Nerva and the word 'putty' do not belong in the same sentence."

"Well, you have 'Aunt' Myrtle now," said Rick, "and she scares people, too. So, it's kind of even."

"Not hardly," said Elizabeth as she handed him a stack of the response cards and a letter opener.

"Really?" asked Rick. "Name me some men in this town who aren't afraid of Mrs. Hod-, I mean, Myrtle."

"My Uncle Deke," said Elizabeth.

"Other than him," said Rick.

"Charlie and Jackson," said Elizabeth.

"I said men, not children," said Rick. "Your nephews are like six and one."

"My dad gets along with her," said Elizabeth.

"Ok, we'll sit her between your dad and Deke," said Rick. "There's your first entry for the seating chart." He pointed at a piece of paper with a mock-up of the clubhouse dining space.

"I was debating between sitting them with mom and dad or with Lucas and Julia. You know how close she is with Julia and Little Margaret," said Elizabeth.

"How close is she to Lucas?" Rick asked.

"You couldn't resist saying that, could you?" asked Elizabeth. "You know, now that Lucas has been around her as much as he has, he does very well with her. Since he's been such a good husband to Julia, she dotes a little on him, too."

"What would she do if he ticked off Julia?" asked Rick.

"Oh, let's not find out," said Elizabeth.

Rick opened his first response card. "Hey, this one's from Bridget. She is coming solo."

"She told me," said Elizabeth. She jotted her assistant's name on the 'yes' column.

"Why would she even send the card back?" asked Rick. "She needs to be there. She's one of your bridesmaids."

"That's my doing," said Elizabeth. "I asked everyone, including my family, to send back the cards. I was afraid that in the chaos of doing all these things," she held up her guest list, "that I would forget to put in some of the most important people. I've seen it happen, and it can get pretty ugly."

Rick shook his head. "I'm glad you thought of that. We have enough drama in the form of our aunts, not to mention you'll want to pour extra amounts of your kindness into my cousin, Melissa."

"Wait, wait, wait!" Elizabeth said in rapid succession. "You had me ask her to be a bridesmaid, and now you are telling me she's hard to handle? Oh, good grief, Rick. I will have enough to think about for our wedding without coddling her."

"'Coddle' is the wrong word, Bets," said Rick, "and you are going to love her."

Elizabeth stared at him. She let out a breath. "Then, what's the issue?"

"She grew up in her older sister's shadow," said Rick. "Her older sister got the attention, and I mean almost all of it. Trisha was the golden girl who was a pageant winner, head cheerleader, etc. She loved the spotlight, and it loved her."

"Melissa must have done some notable things over the years," said Elizabeth.

"Sure, but they never measured up to what Trisha was doing. Melissa made the drill team. Trisha was the head cheerleader. Melissa was Junior Varsity in volleyball. TrishaTrish went to State. The list goes on."

"I'm sorry that happened to her," said Elizabeth. "but how much do I need to do to make her feel comfortable?"

"Just make sure to tell her she looks beautiful in her dress and that you are glad she could be part of the wedding," said Rick. "She will be a wonderful bridesmaid. She's really a sweet person. She does need to know that she has value outside of being Trisha's sister."

"How do you think Trisha reacted to Melissa being asked to be our bridesmaid and not her?" asked Elizabeth.

"I'm sure she's a little irritated with me," said Rick. "Then again, if she thinks about it, and she might or might not, she will know that I was one of the few people who always spent more time talking to Melissa at get-togethers."

"You don't like your cousin, Trisha?" asked Elizabeth.

"I like her just fine," said Rick. "However, I would much rather spend time with Melissa."

"Why?" asked Elizabeth.

"Well," said Rick, "let me put it to you this way. In my opinion, they are both good people, but Trisha had so many accolades, she never learned to put the light on others. Melissa has done little but that over her life. From my point of view, whoever marries Melissa will have a beautiful wife who will be devoted to him and their family. Whoever marries Trisha will have an equally beautiful wife, but one who will be high maintenance. Trisha is used to getting her own way."

"Ah," said Elizabeth. "Well, I think Melissa and I will get along fine."

"You will," said Rick. "Since she doesn't know you well, you will need to draw her out a little. She's used to being quiet and staying in the background."

"I wouldn't need to do that with Trisha?" asked Elizabeth.

"Um, no," said Rick, "she will gladly lead the Conga line during the reception. Melissa will join in if someone asks."

Elizabeth smiled. "Ok, so with whom do I seat Miss Trisha?"

"Put her with Cousin Eugene," said Rick. "Nobody outdoes Geno in the 'I am here' department. Plus, he is quite good at making her feel gorgeous *and* putting her in her place."

"Special skills," said Elizabeth.

"Most definitely," said Rick.

Elizabeth made more notes on her paper. "We need to get back to the actual responses. I'm getting people on here for which I haven't seen for sure if they're coming."

He reached in his back pants pocket and pulled out his wallet. He removed a folded piece of paper. "My side has been calling me ever since we sent the invitations," he said. "Most of them said they would send the cards back anyway, but I think some of the single guys figured they could call and forget about the mail."

"I will never understand men," said Elizabeth.

"Men streamline things," said Rick. "One phone call. Save a stamp. Save a tree. All done."

"I'm surprised they bothered with the phone call," said Elizabeth. "I wouldn't put it past them to text an answer."

Rick cleared his throat.

"No!" said Elizabeth. "Someone actually did that?!"

"Three of them," said Rick.

Elizabeth closed her eyes. "Where's the beauty in that? Some people may put these little cards in their scrapbooks. A folded piece of notebook paper and screen shots of texts aren't exactly the same."

"I know, but at least they let us know," said Rick.

"That's true," said Elizabeth.

"Uh-oh," said Rick as he opened another envelope.

"Uh-oh what?" asked Elizabeth.

"Cousin Eugene is coming in four days early," said Rick.

"I know you said he's a super nice guy," said Elizabeth, "but why? And where is he staying for those four nights?"

"It says here that he wants to make sure to get some beautiful outdoor shots of all the wedding venues," said Rick.

"That's sweet," said Elizabeth, "but why four days?"

"In case there's rain." Rick ran his hand across his face. "Apparently, he asked my dad if he could stay at his place."

"Didn't your dad say anything to you about that?" asked Elizabeth.

"I know he said some of the family is staying there, but he didn't say exactly who or for how long," said Rick. "I just assumed it was for the weekend itself; not the majority of the week."

A look of fright came across Elizabeth's face.

"Bets, what's the matter?" asked Rick. "You look positively petrified!"

"Where is your Aunt Nerva staying?" asked Elizabeth.

"I'm not sure," said Rick. "She's probably going to room with her oldest daughter and one of the granddaughters."

"What's the daughter's name?" asked Elizabeth.

"Chiara Travesti, why?" asked Rick.

Elizabeth ran to her computer and scanned her upcoming reservations. "No!"

"You're not telling me she's staying here?" said Rick.

"If she's rooming with 'Chiara Travesti, party of three' she is," said Elizabeth. "Please tell me Chiara has a husband or another daughter who is coming."

"Well, most of Zietta Nerva's kids are coming," said Rick, "but they are all married right now except for Chiara. She divorced her husband a couple of years ago. Long story. Not pretty, and you don't want to know."

"It looks like they are coming in on Friday and leaving on Monday," said Elizabeth.

"See?" said Rick. "You won't even be here most of that time. You'll be busy all day during the day. Friday, we've got the rehearsal dinner."

"That's at night," said Elizabeth.

"I thought you were going to spend that day with your bridesmaids," said Rick.

"Yes, but she's still staying at *my* property, and she's bound to find something wrong with it," said Elizabeth.

"Bets, if you don't want her to walk all over you, you need to do two things," said Rick.

"What are they?" asked Elizabeth.

"First, look adoringly at me," said Rick, "Zietta wants every in-law to be truly in love with the Polisari they are marrying."

"I think I can handle that," said Elizabeth. "What's the second thing?"

"Tell her you would like to taste her linguine with clam sauce when we next get together," said Rick.

"I love yours," said Elizabeth. "Is it your aunt's recipe?"

"It's the entire family's recipe, but everyone tells her that hers is the best," said Rick.

"Ah," said Elizabeth as she nodded her head. "So, she's not just the family matriarch, but the family chef as well?"

"She's the family's everything," said Rick, "and we all love her. Once her mom and dad passed, she took the role of head of the family quite seriously. She will only acquiesce to her younger brother, Carlo."

"Was she the oldest child?" asked Elizabeth.

"Yes."

"Why does she acquiesce to Carlo?" asked Elizabeth.

"He's the only son," said Rick.

"What about the other sisters?" asked Elizabeth.

"Nope, they just do their thing and let Nerva take the lead," said Rick.

"So, is there anyone I shouldn't seat with Aunt Nerva?" asked Elizabeth.

"My family knows how to handle her," said Rick. "So, I would surround her with my relatives."

Elizabeth scribbled some notes on her paper. "Got it."

Chapter Eight

Bridget swept first, and then used a handheld vacuum on every surface of Examination Room 2 of the clinic. "Those rabbits sure left enough hair in here," she said.

Elizabeth laughed. "Every time they come into the office, I wind up using multiple strips of lint remover tape. They're sweet, though. So, no complaints." She continued to put the strips of tape on her lab coat while talking to her assistant.

"I wasn't complaining either until I started cleaning this room," Bridget said.

"You can't fool me," said Elizabeth. "If you had your own house right now, I can picture you having one or two of them as pets. I see how much you enjoy them."

Bridget laughed. "I'm an animal nut. What can I say?"

She took a break from her vacuuming and looked at her boss. "I will say, though, that I don't know if I would want to clean this all the time."

"I understand," said Elizabeth.

Bridget finished up in the room, discarded her rubber gloves, and washed her hands. "So, what do you and Rick have planned for this weekend? Anything exciting?"

Elizabeth finished her fur removal process and removed her white coat. She noticed more hair had gotten under the coat and onto her black sweater. She gave a little laugh as she took one more piece of tape from the roll and dabbed at the remaining pieces of errant fur.

"Not too much," said Elizabeth. "He's working, of course,

and we are booked solid for the weekend here at the B & B. It will be another typical weekend in the lives of Rick Polisari and Elizabeth Anderson."

She smiled at her assistant. "What about you?"

"Not a whole lot," said Bridget. "I think I am going to take advantage of the day tomorrow, and head out to your folks' campground."

"You plan on going to the diner?" said Elizabeth.

"The autumn colors are starting to peak," said Bridget. "I thought I would walk the campground trails and enjoy them. You always say that makes you feel whole and rested when you go out there. Why don't you go, too?"

Elizabeth put her head back and stretched. "It's not that I couldn't use some relaxation right now. This has been a crazy, busy week here. I mean, every room we have in the bed and breakfast has been filled. Our veterinary schedule has been full. We even added extra hours to the patient appointment times, and we still had people waiting to get in!"

"That's because they know the clinic will be closed for almost two weeks for your wedding and honeymoon!" said Bridget.

"I have a back-up veterinarian," said Elizabeth.

"True," said Bridget, "but he is not you. So, if it's something that can be done while you're around, heck, I would book it, too."

Elizabeth stretched again. "I should be flattered by that, I guess."

"Yes, you should," said Bridget. Her voice held a firmness that said she meant it.

"I'm just tired, Bridget," said Elizabeth.

Bridget came over and stood next to her. She pulled one of the waiting room chairs closer to Elizabeth and pointed for her to sit down.

"I have three things to say to you right now," said Bridget.

"What are they?" asked Elizabeth.

"Number one," said Bridget, "do you remember your deal with Rick about not stretching yourself too thin?"

Elizabeth closed her eyes for a second. "Yes."

"Number two," said Bridget, "do you remember that both your sister, Angela and I offered to do a lot of this arranging and chasing for your wedding things for you?"

"Yes."

"Well, when are you going to start listening to your body and your mind?" asked Bridget. "You're exhausted right now. You know you have a tendency to run yourself into the ground so that everything gets done – and – you don't like to ask for help."

"That was many months ago," said Elizabeth.

"And it's now, too," said Bridget. "You aren't alienating people the way you were then, but you still haven't learned how to let other people help. You don't need to be a one-woman show, Elizabeth!"

Elizabeth was silent for a moment. "I haven't thought about it much, but that's not my goal."

"You're acting as though it is," said Bridget.

"I don't like how this conversation is heading," said Elizabeth.

"Look," said Bridget, "I'm seeing it. My guess is that soon everyone else will, or that you will wind up letting yourself slide so far again that you will start barking at Rick or making other people feel unwanted."

"You don't pull any punches, do you?" asked Elizabeth.

"No," said Bridget. "I'm a stubborn Irish woman. Be glad you have me around. Other people would let you think you are perfect."

"I'm not perfect," said Elizabeth. "I hate when people call me that."

"Then quit trying to have everyone think you are," said Bridget. "Say 'no' once in a while when people ask you to expand your schedule one more time."

Elizabeth stretched one more time. "Bridget, I'm tired."

"Well, so am I!" said Bridget. "Every time you expand your schedule, mine expands with it."

"Oh, Bridget, I'm sorry!" said Elizabeth. "I never want you to feel that you have to be here every time I have a patient, nor do I expect you to take on anything extra with the B & B. You do more than your job already, and you have since the day you got here."

Bridget rubbed her neck and then looked Elizabeth in the eyes. "Yeah, well, I do feel I should be here when there are clients, and I do want to help you with the B & B. I also want to help you with your wedding."

"You would be adding more to your list," said Elizabeth. "You just said you were tired. How can I do that to you?"

Bridget sighed. "Think of it this way, I'm one of your closest friends."

"That's true," said Elizabeth.

"Yes, and I want to be here for you in any way that I can make your life easier, more efficient, or more fun," said Bridget. "So, let's figure out a way for me to do that without us both keeling over from exhaustion."

Chapter Nine

"I'm getting static from Bridget again," said Elizabeth into her phone. She put her feet up on the little ottoman she had next to the chair in her bedroom.

"For what?" asked Rick as he munched on a post-work piece of pizza.

"What are you eating?" asked Elizabeth. "I can hear you chewing."

Rick swallowed. "Sorry, I didn't get a chance to grab supper earlier, and I am famished. It's pepperoni and anchovies. Someone ordered it and never picked it up. So, it's *my* supper now."

"Oh, well, I'd tell you I'd come over and share it with you, but I'm not much for anchovies," said Elizabeth.

"You don't fool me," said Rick. "You'll be in bed in half an hour."

"True," said Elizabeth, "but it was a momentary thought."

"So, what was Bridget upset about?" asked Rick. He took another bite.

"She says I'm spreading myself too thin again," said Elizabeth.

"This time, it's only temporary," said Rick. "Once the wedding is over, life will get back to a regular pace."

"Except for going back and forth between your place and mine," said Elizabeth.

"That's temporary, too," said Rick.

Elizabeth sighed.

"Look, Bets," said Rick, "if this is going to stress you out, I will just move in with you at Yarkton House."

"We talked about that, too, Rick," said Elizabeth. "There's precious little privacy here."

"Honey," said Rick, "I will live wherever you want, whenever you want, but I will *not* live in separate houses. This marriage is a commitment for me, but I need to be honest here. This is a 'husband and wife' thing for me, not an extended dating relationship."

"I didn't ask for it to be," said Elizabeth.

"Good, because I want you to be my wife," said Rick.

"Would that be why you asked me to marry you?" asked Elizabeth with a laugh.

"That, and a few other reasons. Truth, Bets?" said Rick.

"Please."

"I'm getting a little sick of this 'dating' thing.

"Yeah," said Elizabeth. "It does sort of have an expiration date on it, doesn't it?"

"It does for me," said Rick. "I wanted us to be married a long time ago. The waiting is starting to get to me."

"It's two weeks from today," said Elizabeth, "and today is almost over."

"Thank God," said Rick.

"I love you, Rick," said Elizabeth.

"That's good," said Rick, "because I love you, too."

There was a moment of silence in the conversation.

"Rick?" said Elizabeth.

"I'm here," he said.

"Something else Bridget said bothered me," said Elizabeth.

"What was that?" asked Rick.

Elizabeth blew out a long breath. "She said that every time I expand my own schedule, hers expands, too. I never thought about that. I never meant to put more on Bridget; just myself."

"Do you demand she be in the clinic every time you are there?" asked Rick.

"No," said Elizabeth, "but she knows when I am there, and she feels like she's slacking if she doesn't come in and help."

"What about the Sunday breakfasts?" asked Rick. "Did you ever tell her she had to do those?"

"You know the answer to that, Rick," said Elizabeth, "she offered. In fact, she darn near forced me to let her be a part of those. She's even the one who organizes the other volunteers."

"And what about all the stuff she's doing for the wedding?" asked Rick. "Did you tell her she had to do that?"

"Well, of course not!" said Elizabeth. "Bridget said she and Angela want to help."

"You're not getting my point, are you, Bets?" asked Rick.

"I'm not sure," said Elizabeth.

"Bets," said Rick, "yes, you are taking on a lot right now, and while I do understand what a good friend Bridget is being by taking on more and more to help you, the fact is that *she* is the one taking it on herself. You are not making her expand her schedule at all. She just *feels* as though you are."

"I guess I understand that," said Elizabeth, "but how do I say that to her without hurting her feelings?"

"If the subject comes up again," said Rick, "you'll think of a way. Hopefully, once the wedding is over-"

"Why do you keep saying that?" Elizabeth interjected.

"What do you mean?" asked Rick.

"You keep saying, 'once the wedding is over,'" said Elizabeth.

"Yes, and?" said Rick.

"It sounds like you *want* it to be over," said Elizabeth, "that you aren't looking forward to our actual wedding day!"

"Well, there's a leap," said Rick.

"Come again?" said Elizabeth.

"I want to be your husband," said Rick.

"You've said that," said Elizabeth.

"Well," said Rick, "how do you think that happens?"

"By getting married," said Elizabeth, "you know, having an actual wedding ceremony."

"And when are we actually considered 'husband and wife?'" asked Rick.

"Once Pastor Plain has us say, 'I do,'" said Elizabeth.

"Does that happen at the beginning or the end of the service?" asked Rick.

"The end, of course," said Elizabeth.

"Yes, it does," said Rick. "So, my dear, sweet, love of my entire life, I do want to have the wedding. I want to see you in your gorgeous dress. I want to see you smile as you walk down the aisle to me. I want to hold your hand. Give you our wedding kiss, and I want to take in every moment of that day possible. I want to tell my memories of that day to anyone who will listen. Our great-grandchildren will be bored to tears when I repeat those stories for the hundredth time to them."

"Ok," said Elizabeth, "you made your point. You can stop now."

"Please don't ever say that I am not excited about our wedding ever again," said Rick.

"I won't, "said Elizabeth.

"Good," said Rick. "Now, get some sleep, and stop worrying about everything. It will all be fine."

Chapter Ten

Bridget pulled her small, bright blue car into the Pineville Diner and Campground parking lot. The lot was large, with truck and motorcycle parking in addition to the ample spots for regular cars. She chose a spot close to the campground entrance. "I haven't walked these trails since you took me out here that one summer," she said.

Elizabeth peered through Bridget's car's windshield. She looked up at the sky. "There are some clouds," she said, "but I don't think it will rain on us."

Bridget opened her car door and grabbed her jacket from the back seat. "Nah, it wouldn't rain on us today. I have a good feeling about that."

"You're certainly optimistic this morning," said Elizabeth.

Bridget shrugged. "I guess I just know it's going to be a wonderful day."

"I hope you're right," said Elizabeth.

"Oh, for heaven's sake, Elizabeth," said Bridget. "Quit dawdling. Let's get walking. There are trees to be seen!" She gestured with her hand to catch up to her.

Elizabeth chuckled.

There was much that intertwined the lives of Elizabeth Anderson and Bridget O'Dunn. They talked of the wedding, the clinic, the bed and breakfast, plans for the attic renovations, and life in general. They spoke of their time together in Madison, where they had met about five years earlier. Conversations went from family to friends to work and to nature.

There were many moments of silence as they took in the beauty of the campground in its early autumnal stage.

The leaves had erupted with color, showing off their fall majesty. Deep ruby reds combined with splendid oranges and yellows that rivaled the sun's. The remaining green leaves provided backdrop for the glory of autumn's show.

Soaring birds called from overhead with caws, chirps, and whistles letting the two women know that they were surrounded by wonderful sights and sounds of God's creation.

They heard the river before they saw it. The clouds had not produced rain, but the wind had escalated, and the river responded with a louder voice.

"Wow," said Bridget as she walked to the water's edge. "Look at that! I've never seen whitecaps on a river before."

"It doesn't happen all that often," said Elizabeth, "but when it does, it's a clear sign to stay out of the water. That current can get dangerous even when the weather is fairly stable. You add this to the mix, and you have a recipe for disaster. It's treacherous."

"I'm sorry, Elizabeth," said Bridget. "I didn't mean to upset you. I thought it was beautiful to see."

"You didn't upset me," said Elizabeth, "and it is quite beautiful. However, beautiful things can also be dangerous.

"Did you want to go back?" asked Bridget.

Elizabeth shook her head no. "As long as we don't put our feet in the water and stay back from the slippery ground around it, we'll be fine."

They picked a large oak tree about twenty feet from the banks of the Huhawira and sat down to watch the river's fast flow and listen to the sound of the rushing waters.

A while later, Bridget stood up and checked her cell phone. "I'd like to head back now if you don't mind. I have a couple of things to do yet this afternoon."

Elizabeth rose. "Absolutely. Anything I can help you with?"

"Only one thing," said Bridget.

"What's that?" asked Elizabeth.

"Could we make a quick pit stop at the clubhouse?" asked Bridget. "I'd like to take one more look at it for some decorating ideas for the wedding. Angela and I are going to do the shopping for that this week."

"Not a problem," said Elizabeth. "Believe it or not, I actually have a quiet day with no other plans."

"Surprise!" yelled out a group of people as Elizabeth and Bridget came in the front door of the campground's clubhouse.

"What?!" said Elizabeth.

"Happy wedding shower!" said Bridget.

"I thought surprise showers were a thing of the past," said Elizabeth.

"Nope," said Bridget, "besides, you always like things steeped in tradition."

"That's true," said Elizabeth.

Bridget nudged her in the back. "You had better get mingling. You have a lot of guests."

As Elizabeth came further into the room, Rick stepped out from behind the door. "One more surprise," he said.

Elizabeth threw her arms around his neck. "You're here!" she said.

"I wouldn't miss this for the world," said Rick. "You know how much I need to build those memories for our great-grandchildren."

Elizabeth gave him a sideways glance and shook her head. "You made your point last night."

Rick gave her a short kiss. "And I am still making it today."

"Hey!" shouted one of the younger women. "You guys can do that later. You have guests waiting to see you!"

Rick and Elizabeth laughed.

Bridget looked at Elizabeth. "I told you so."

Rick and Elizabeth made their way through the throng of guests. "If there's this many people at the shower," said Elizabeth, "I'm not sure we'll fit the entire wedding crowd in here."

"Don't worry," said Rick, "your mom is a pro at setting up this room."

"Well," said Elizabeth, "that's certainly true."

They approached a table that held some of their church friends, plus Myrtle and Deke. "Hi, everyone," said Elizabeth.

"When did men start getting invited to these things?" asked Deke. "I thought only women did this."

"Ssshhh," said Myrtle. "It's the new way, Deke. Be polite."

"Well, it can be either way now, Uncle Deke," said Elizabeth. "It depends on who plans the party."

"Hm," Deke said sharply, "Angela and Bridget, two young ladies who don't realize us old men don't feel comfortable at these things."

A group of men on the other side of the room erupted in laughter.

"Apparently *some* men are finding it fun," said Myrtle. "Then again, *some* men want to spend time with their wives."

Rick and Elizabeth froze. Neither one knew what to say.

"Now, Myrt," said Deke, "you know I love spending all the time I can with you."

"So you say," said Myrtle.

"You know I do, Sweetheart," said Deke.

"Well, I see someone waving to us," said Rick. "We'd better get moving. Thanks again for coming, everyone. Bets and I sure appreciate it."

The young couple began to walk to the next table.

"Who was waving at us?" asked Elizabeth.

"No one," said Rick.

Elizabeth nodded.

By the time they made it around the room, caterers were bringing in silver serving dishes full of pulled pork, shredded beef, black bean burgers, and an array of side dishes designed to whet anyone's appetite.

"Oh, my goodness, you guys," Elizabeth said to Bridget and Angela, "you did way too much! That's a lot of food."

"I've worked in the diner almost all my life," said Angela. "I think I know how to order food for a group."

"Anj," said Elizabeth, "there's got to be enough food to feed almost twice as many people as are here."

"That's true," said Angela, "but a number of the husbands didn't come. I want to make sure there's enough food for their wives to take home plates for them."

"So, Uncle Deke isn't the only one who didn't want to be here?" asked Elizabeth.

"No," said Angela, "but almost all of the ones that did come are having a blast!"

"For most of them," said Bridget, "they've been invited to showers before. For some of them, they want to see what's behind the curtain."

"Behind the curtain?" asked Elizabeth.

"Yes," said Bridget. "Some of these guys think women have a secret code or something; that we are hiding something from them when we go to these parties. Once they find out it's not all cucumber sandwiches, lady fingers, and tea, they're fine."

"Excuse me," said Angela, "I think it's time to get people to the tables. The men are starting to drool, and I think I see one or two of the ladies getting snacks out of their purses."

"That's not good," said Elizabeth.

Angela took the microphone from the head table and blew into it to make sure it was on. "Good afternoon, everyone!"

A chorus of 'good afternoons' came back to her.

"I want to thank you again for coming today to honor my sister, Elizabeth, and her handsome fiancé, Rick."

Elizabeth wished Angela hadn't referred to Rick as 'handsome.' She knew it, of course, but she didn't want anyone else to focus on that.

"I'm not going to give a big speech here, because I am not the guest of honor. However, I do want to take a moment to say thank you to the many people who helped with this party. To the other bridesmaids, especially Bridget, who is the other person that set this up, and to my family who always pitches in wherever needed. Thank you."

She handed the microphone to Bridget.

Bridget looked out at the room. "Angela hit the exact same points I was going to make. First, nobody wants long speeches from me, either. Second, thank you all for coming. Third, thank you to everyone whose hands were here to help – especially when I was busy keeping Elizabeth away from here."

Some light laughter was scattered throughout the clubhouse.

"I do want thank Angela, my co-conspirator. We did it, Anj! We truly surprised her!"

Angela nodded in ascent. "Yes, I think we did."

"I also thank Angela for having a truly awesome sister," said Bridget, "and with that said, I am going to give this microphone to Elizabeth."

"Oh, my goodness," said Elizabeth. "You're coming up there with me, Rick."

"No, this is for you," said Rick.

Elizabeth shook her head no. "This is for *us*." She reached for his hand and tugged until he stood and walked with her.

Clapping greeted them at the mic stand.

"Thank you, everybody," said Elizabeth. She held the microphone between herself and Rick.

"Absolutely," said Rick.

"You know, Rick and I have been so blessed throughout our lives," said Elizabeth. "Not only do we now have each other, but we have each of you. Your presence here today means more than you may know."

She pushed the mic closer to Rick. "I feel the same as Elizabeth."

Elizabeth encouraged him to say something else.

He took the microphone from her hand. "Ok," he said, "I guess this is something most husbands-to-be feel, but I believe I am getting the most beautiful, and loving woman in the world for my wife. We all know how hard she works in her businesses, whether that's at her vet clinic or with Yarkton House. Well, folks, she works just that hard on her personal life. She always lets me know I am loved. She is kind, caring, and honest. You don't always find all of that in one person. I got lucky."

With that, he put the mic back on the stand and said, "Let's eat!" The men in the room applauded loudly.

"That was beautiful, Rick," said Angela.

"Thank you," said Rick.

"You guys should be the first to eat," said Bridget, "and you had better get up there before those guys in the back stampede the meat line."

"You don't have to tell me twice," said Rick. "I'm hungry, and I didn't have to cook it for myself. That's a win-win for me."

On their way back to the head table, they passed the dessert and gift tables. The crowning glory in the center of it all was a tiered cake with fresh flowers on the top.

"I don't even have to ask who made that decorated cake," said Rick.

"Aunt Bonnie has made almost every decorated cake for this family since before I was born," said Elizabeth.

"That's an advantage of having a baker in the family," said Rick. "There's never a question where you should place your order."

"Or if she can fit it in her schedule," said Elizabeth.

"Those cupcakes around the bottom look good, too," said Rick. "I might have to sample both the cake and the cupcakes. I wouldn't want to miss out on something from this day."

"Ha-ha," said Elizabeth, "you just want two desserts."

"Well, maybe," said Rick, "but don't tell anyone else. It will destroy my healthy image."

Once the meal was over and the cake served, Rick and Elizabeth were ushered to two chairs where they would open their presents.

"Do you want to start with the cards or the boxes?" asked Angela as they sat.

Angela had the duties of handing them the gifts, one-by-one, while Bridget kept the notes as to who gave what.

"Let's do the cards," said Elizabeth.

Angela sat a decorated box on her sister's lap. "Here you go!" she said.

Elizabeth opened the top of the box. Several envelopes were inside. "Holy smokes," said Elizabeth. "There are a lot of cards in here!"

"That's why we made a box," said Angela. "We didn't want any to get lost in the room or somehow get mixed with the wrong gift."

"That definitely would not be good," said Elizabeth.

Elizabeth and Rick made their way through the cards. They spent a bit of time on each one, reading the scripted inside and thanking each person for their thoughtfulness. The last card in the box was from Aunt Bonnie. 'I hope you like the cake,' was written inside.

"I knew it was from you!" said Rick.

"However did you guess?" asked Bonnie.

The guests laughed as the couple began on the boxes of presents.

"This one is from me," said Angela.

Elizabeth took her time unwrapping the large box. When she peeled back the tissue paper, a white, beautifully knitted, cable-stitch blanket was unveiled. "Oh, Anj," said Elizabeth, "you've really gotten good at knitting! It's fantastic!" She handed the box and blanket to Rick and stood to hug her sister.

Rick held the blanket up so the guests could get a better look at it. A number of the people closest to the gift area oohed and aahed.

"Angela, you'd better take this and put it back in the box for now," said Rick. "I'm afraid if I hold on to it, I'll drop it or something."

"No problem," said Angela.

"We want to see it, too!" yelled someone from the back of the room.

"Don't worry," said Bridget, "Angela and I will have everything set out at the end so you can see it all."

"Thank you!" yelled another person.

Angela took the blanket box and handed Elizabeth the next present from the stack.

It took nearly a half hour to open all the boxes.

"This one doesn't have a card on it," said Angela as she handed it to Elizabeth.

"It might be inside," said Elizabeth. As she unwrapped the box, she looked to see if there was a card attached to the outside of the box. Seeing none, she opened the box. Again, she found no card.

She unwrapped the many layers of tissue. When she arrived at the gift, she let out a gasp. "Oh, wow. These are beautiful!"

Rick said, "They are stunning!" He held one of them up, and there were gasps and wows from the crowd as well. "Sorry, folks," he said, "but we can't find a card with these. Could whomever gave us these incredible candlesticks let us know who you are?"

People turned their heads from side-to-side, but no one's hand was raised.

Rick asked Bridget to bring him the microphone from the center table. He turned it on and said again, "I don't know if those of you in the back could hear me, but we are looking to thank the person who gave us these gorgeous candlesticks."

Still, no one responded.

Rick handed the microphone back to Bridget and said quietly to Elizabeth, "These look expensive. I wonder why no one is saying anything."

"Maybe they were sent in the mail from someone who couldn't attend," said Elizabeth.

"If these are from some folks in my family, the other contributors are going to be extremely unhappy when they find out there was no card," said Rick.

"I hope someone says something at the wedding," said Elizabeth. "I'd hate not to be able to thank the person who took the time to find these and gift them to us."

"Not to mention the cost," said Rick.

Elizabeth nodded as Angela handed her the next gift. "I'm

not sure I even want to know what the price was," she said to Rick as she continued on with the rest of the presents.

When the couple had finished opening their gifts, Bridget said, "Bonnie said to let you know that there is cake left for anyone who would like to take a slice home with them. The cupcakes are gone, though."

There were a few groans over the no-longer-available cupcakes.

"I'll have more in the shop on Tuesday!" said Bonnie.

"I think I will have to stop in that day for a little breakfast," said Rick.

"You must know Michael," said Bonnie. "You and him could have a 'sweet-talking' contest."

"I'll win!" shouted Michael from across the room.

"I wouldn't bet on that!" said Rick.

"We're talking about Aunt Bonnie's cupcakes here, Rick," said Michael. "I've had years of experience telling her how delicious they are."

"You forget, Michael," said Rick. "I'm older than you are, and I've grown up on the Pineville Bakery, too."

"Not as much as I have," said Michael.

"Don't argue, boys," said Bonnie. "I'll put one aside for each of you on Tuesday."

"Thank you, Aunt Bonnie," said both Michael and Rick.

Later that evening, Rick and Elizabeth snuggled on the couch at his apartment.

"Were you really surprised today?" asked Rick.

"Oh, yes," said Elizabeth, "I didn't have a clue."

"I'm glad," said Rick. "I think Bridget could have gone either way with the 'surprise' part, but it was really important to Angela that it be one."

"She's such a wonderful sister," said Elizabeth, "and Bridget is one terrific friend."

"It was a fun party," said Rick. "You know, even your Uncle

Deke started to warm up to it."

"Myrtle may have had something to do with that," said Elizabeth.

"Yes, well, she did let him know she didn't like his original attitude about it," said Rick. He laughed at the memory.

"There's no doubt about that," said Elizabeth. She snuggled in closer to her fiancé. "Are you going to want to do things with me after we're married?"

"Don't I now?" asked Rick.

She tilted her face up toward his. "Yes, but now we're engaged. I mean after we're married."

"Bets," said Rick, "one thing about me, what you see is what you get. The only changes I have planned for our relationship once we're married is to make it even deeper and closer."

A slow smile came across Elizabeth's face. "Can I hold you to that?"

<h1 style="text-align:center">Chapter Eleven</h1>

Pineville Community Church's Fellowship Hall was filled with parishioners enjoying a cup of coffee or a doughnut. The hour before the Sunday morning service had become a welcome time for the churchgoers to visit with fellow members and catch up on each other's weeks.

"Oh, dear," said Barbara as she and her husband made their entrance into the basement room. "The Andersons' tables are already full. I told you we should have left earlier, Johnny."

"Barbara, how early would you have had us leave?" her husband asked. "We pulled out of Milwaukee well before dawn as it was. I'm tired, and we haven't even started unloading that truck."

Their son, Tim, came in a minute later. "Why are you standing here?"

Barbara pointed in the direction of the Anderson tables. "Look, there's no room there. We're going to have to sit with someone else."

"Maybe," said Tim. He walked over to the Andersons.

"Good morning, everyone!" he said.

Stephanie got up from her seat and gave her brother a hug. "Tim! I didn't expect you guys until *after* church. What time did you leave the house?"

"Don't ask," said Tim. "I'm in the house of God. I don't want to tell you what I was thinking when Mom got me up at four o'clock."

Stephanie smiled. "Mom didn't want to miss her first Sunday

morning in Pineville?"

Tim gave her a momentary glare. "Mom doesn't want to miss out if anyone in Pineville even has a hangnail. Good luck to you."

"Are you saying we're going to have a new member in the Pineville Pipeline?" asked Michael.

"What's that?" asked Tim.

Joseph looked at his brother-in-law. "That's what people here call the local gossips."

Tim let out a loud laugh, causing a few nearby folks to look in his direction. "Sorry," he said to them.

He turned back toward the Anderson family. "That's priceless. However, I wouldn't share that with my mom, Michael. She looks at it as being 'concerned.'"

"They all do," said Joseph. He began to rub his forehead.

"What's the matter, Daddy?" asked his seven-year-old daughter, Emmie.

"Nothing, Sweetheart," said Joseph.

"But, Daddy," said Emmie, "you only rub your head when you have a headache, or something is wrong. Don't you feel good?"

"I'm fine," said Joseph. "Why don't you go invite Grandma Barbara to come sit with us?"

Tim went over to an adjacent table that had a few empty chairs. "Do you mind if we borrow these?" he asked the couple who was sitting there.

"Not at all," said the man.

Tim, Joseph, and Michael each grabbed a chair and carried them over to where the Andersons were sitting.

Tim waved to his parents. "Over here."

"Thank you," said Johnny and Barbara.

"Mom, we wouldn't dream of letting you sit with someone else," said Stephanie, "especially not on your first Sunday as Pineville residents."

"We don't want to crowd you," said Johnny.

Barbara sat down and immediately pulled one of the twins on her lap. "How's my little angel today?" she cooed to the little one.

"She was content in her seat," said Stephanie.

"She's awake, Stephie," said Barbara. "Grandma hasn't seen you in so long," she said to the baby.

"It's only been a couple of weeks, Mom," said Stephanie.

"Get used to it," said Johnny. "You know your mother."

Joseph started rubbing his forehead again.

It was a short walk after church to Lucas and Julia's charming old home.

"Thank you for offering to keep the kids, Jules," said Stephanie. She handed one of the twins to her as she and Joseph made their way into the living room.

"Uncle Lucas," said six-year-old Charlie, "can you take me fishing this afternoon?"

"Not today, Charlie," said Lucas. "We need to stay here and help Auntie Julia with the little ones."

"How come there are so many babies in this family?" asked Charlie.

Lucas chuckled. "Because we're very blessed."

Charlie's response didn't sound enthusiastic. "Oh, ok. I wish God would bless us with a dog, though."

"You can play with Sniffy," said Stephanie.

"But, he's Auntie Elizabeth's dog! He's not mine," said Charlie.

"That's right," said Joseph, "and if you keep whining, you won't be playing with him, either."

Charlie started to pout, but the look on his father's face told him that was not a good idea. "I'm sorry, Daddy."

"That's better," said Joseph. Joseph bent over to Charlie's level. "Now, listen. Your mom and I are going to be very busy today helping your grandma and grandpa move into their new house. I need you to behave and help Uncle Lucas and Aunt Julia as much as possible. Do you understand me?"

Charlie nodded.

"Ok," said Joseph. "I don't want to hear anything different when I get back. Do you understand that, too?"

"Yes," said Charlie.

"Joseph," said Stephanie, "we'd better go. You know how Mom gets when someone is late. She'll think we had an accident or something."

Joseph rubbed the back of his neck.

"Does your neck hurt, too, now, Daddy?" asked Emmie.

"Daddy will be fine," said Stephanie. "We just have a lot to do today."

"Auntie Julia, do you think we can bake cookies today?" asked Charlie.

"Charlie!" said Joseph.

"We've got this, Joseph," said Lucas. "Go. We wouldn't want to make you late for the move."

"Did I detect a note of laughter in your voice, Lucas?" asked Joseph. "You sounded a lot like Michael when you said that."

Stephanie touched her husband's arm. "We really *should* go."

"I know," said Joseph.

"Bye," said Lucas.

When Joseph glared at him, Lucas's face broke into a full smile.

"Tell your parents I am sorry we couldn't be there to help them today," said Julia.

"You *are* helping them," said Stephanie. "You're watching the kids."

"I know," said Julia, "but you know what I mean. Your folks have always been there for me."

"We'll be seeing them tonight at the house for dinner, right, Steph?" asked Lucas.

Joseph groaned and rubbed his forehead again.

"Daddy, do you need some medicine for your headache?" asked Emmie.

"No, he's fine, Emmie," said Stephanie.

She turned her attention to her husband. "I am getting in the car now, Joseph, and you'd better be two steps behind me."

Lucas stifled a laugh.

The look Joseph gave his brother was scathing, which made

Lucas burst out in a long, loud laugh.

"Lucas," said Julia, "I'm not sure I've ever heard you laugh like that before."

After Joseph and Stephanie finally made their way out the door, Julia looked at her husband. "Most people would cringe at that look he gave you."

"Julia, you forget, I've had many years of practice dealing with Joseph's moods and looks," said Lucas. "That's one advantage of being his brother."

"Is he really that stressed out about Stephanie's parents moving here?" asked Julia. "He's known they were looking for a place since before the twins were born."

"Yes," said Lucas, "well, it's one thing for them to be looking, and something completely different for them to actually have the moving truck sitting in front of the new place."

"Doesn't Daddy want Grandpa Johnny and Grandma Barbara here?" asked Emmie.

Julia and Lucas look wide-eyed at each other.

"Oh, no, Emmie," said Julia, "that's not it. Your daddy wants to make sure they are happy here."

"Why wouldn't they be happy?" asked Emmie.

"They will be," said Julia.

"Emmie," said Lucas, "can you and Charlie run out in the backyard and bring in a few more toys for the little ones from the bin out there?"

"Sure," said Emmie. "Come on, Charlie."

When the two older children were out of earshot, Julia said, "I forgot how much they pick up. I am such a dolt!"

"No," said Lucas. "You're just used to having a one-year-old in the house and not a six and almost eight-year-old."

"I am going to have to remember that," said Julia. "If Barbara hears that, I could start a war in the Anderson family."

"Don't worry," said Lucas. "We've got Myrtle and Barbara in the same family now. Sooner or later, someone's going to blow."

Julia rubbed her forehead and groaned.

"That headache of Joseph's must be contagious," Lucas said.

"Oh, Stephie!" said Barbara before Stephanie was completely out of the car. "I was getting so worried about you! You're late!"

Stephanie gave her mother a hug. "Only by a few minutes, Mom."

"How packed is that truck, Johnny?" said Joseph. He walked over to the back of it. "I thought the movers were bringing most of this on Tuesday."

"Yes," said Tim. "I did, too. Apparently, Mom absolutely had to have some of this before that."

Joseph gave his neck a quick rub. "Well, I guess we just start and keep going until it's done."

"Oh, dear," said Barbara as she arrived at the back of the truck. "I didn't realize it was this full! How are we ever going to get this all done today? My goodness. I don't know where to put it all. Some of this might need furniture that's still at home."

"Barbara Lu," said Johnny, "let's get started, and worry about the details as they arise."

"Mom, why don't you and I go in the house and let the guys know where to put things?" said Stephanie.

Barbara kept looking back at the open truck from over her shoulder as Stephanie steered her toward the inside of the house.

"Hey, Joseph," said Michael.

"Yes."

"I got a text from Lucas," said Michael.

"Is something going on with one of the kids?" asked Joseph.

"No, I guess the kids are fine," said Michael.

"Then, what's up?" asked Joseph.

"He said for me to ask you if your headache is any better or if he should run some aspirin over here," Michael said.

Joseph's face took on the same look he had recently directed at his other brother. "I'm going to kill him," he said under his breath.

"Now, now," said Michael, "you're the sheriff. You know that's illegal."

Joseph's face still had its glare. "Some things are justifiable."

"Jeannie," said Bonnie, "it's a good thing you made dinner in a slow cooker tonight. It would be ruined by now if you hadn't."

Jeannie started splitting the buns for the dinner and putting them into a large bowl. "I kind of figured they would run late. Joseph texted me when he got there and said the truck was absolutely packed to the maximum."

Bonnie started opening all the condiment jars and putting serving knives or forks in them. "How do you think Joseph and Stephanie really feel about her parents moving here?" she asked. "Besides which, how are you feeling about it?"

"Stephanie is thrilled. Joseph will be fine. He will need a bit of adjustment to Barbara's non-stop chatter, but he'll do it. After all, Stephanie used to talk with high-energy, too, and he married her. So, it can't bother him too much."

A few seconds ticked away on the clock.

"Jeannie," said her older sister, "you didn't answer my question."

"Yes, I did."

"Not completely," said Bonnie. "I asked you how you felt about them moving here."

Jeannie stopped cutting the buns for the barbecued beef. She looked at her sister. "It's not about me. This is about Joseph, Stephanie, their children, Johnny, and Barbara."

"Nonsense," said Bonnie, "this is about you, too."

"No, it's not," said Jeannie.

"Oh, yes, it is," said Bonnie. "You have had all of your grandchildren almost exclusively to yourself for all these years. Now, all of a sudden, Myrtle has become 'Grandma Myrtle' to Little Margaret, and 'Grandpa Johnny' and 'Grandma Barbara' have now arrived to be a bigger part of Joseph and Stephanie's children's lives. You are going from solo grandmother of five to sharing those grandchildren. I find it hard to believe that you are coasting through that without any bruised ego whatsoever."

"My ego is not bruised," said Jeannie. "In fact, my ego has nothing to do with it."

"Uh-huh," said Bonnie. "So, everything is peachy, and you never once had any twinge of an ouch or sadness with your role changing."

"My role is not changing!" yelled Jeannie.

Bonnie stepped back from the table and looked her sister in the face. "Then, why did you yell? The last time you yelled at me was when I tripped and dropped a hot pan of brownies on your foot."

"That hurt, you know," said Jeannie. "Thankfully, I was wearing socks and shoes. If I was wearing sandals, my foot would have had a nasty burn."

"Yes, I do know," said Bonnie, "and I know at some level this hurts, too."

"Most people have to share their grandchildren with another side of the family," said Jeannie.

"But you never really did," said her sister. "Plus, you basically raised Emmie and Charlie in those early years after Tracy died and before Joseph married Stephanie."

"Yes," said Jeannie.

"You have never, not ever, had a regular relationship with your grandchildren," said Bonnie. "You've been GRANDMA in big capital letters. No 'Grandma Jeannie' or 'Grandma Anderson.' Just plain Grandma."

"So what?" said Jeannie.

"So, don't tell me this isn't an adjustment for you, too," said Bonnie. "This summer has been filled with upheaval for you."

"No, it hasn't," said Jeannie.

"Oh, yes, it has," said Bonnie. She sat down on a kitchen chair next to Jeannie. "First, Deke marries Myrtle in what has to be some record-setting engagement."

"Yes, but what does that have to do with me?" asked Jeannie.

"Please," Bonnie said. "Who do you think you're talking to? Some stranger in the supermarket? It's me, your sister, and you cannot hide your feelings from me. I've known you too well for too long for that to work."

"Ok, how is that supposed to affect me?" asked Jeannie.

"Because you are not the only wife," said Bonnie.

"I'm Don's only wife, and that's all that matters," said Jeannie.

"Not true," said Bonnie. "You have always been the only female presence for both Don and Deke. They always let you do your thing, handle all the party planning, the scheduling, etc. Now, Myrtle tells Deke where he should be and when. Myrtle makes plans that don't always include you."

"And you think I'm jealous of that?" asked Jeannie.

"Not jealous, but it's different," said Bonnie, "and Myrtle is strong-willed. So, Deke is going to listen to her if he wants to keep a happy home."

"A lot of this family is strong-willed," said Jeannie. "That's nothing new."

"The dynamics are new," said Bonnie.

"Yes, they are, but for the most part, I'm quite happy with that. Deke deserved to find someone to love. Let's face it, Bonnie," said Jeannie, "he wasn't exactly a ladies man all those years. I'm glad to see him be able to do something with someone other than Don, myself, and our kids."

"Thank you," said Bonnie.

"For what?" asked Jeannie.

"You just said, 'for the most part,'" said Bonnie.

"Yes."

"That's my point, Jeannie," said Bonnie. "You may be basically happy for him, but there are still a few adjustments you need to make to keep things going smoothly."

"Ok," said Jeannie, "but don't forget, we've all known each other for most of our lives."

"Yes, but now come the Cannadys. You haven't known them your whole life. In fact, you met them only a few years ago and now, poof, they are Grandma and Grandpa to four of the five grandchildren. I don't know how that affects you with Jackson and Jillian, but Emmie and Charlie pre-date the arrival of

Stephanie's parents by a number of years," said Bonnie.

"I am grateful the twins will have two sets of loving grandparents for their entire lives," said Jeannie.

"And what about the older two?" asked Bonnie.

"I'm happy they have Johnny and Barbara now," said Jeannie.

"And for not so much as one second did you ever have a pang of sadness that you wouldn't be the sole queen in their lives?" asked Bonnie.

"Let's not be so dramatic," said Jeannie.

"You know what I'm saying," said Bonnie.

Jeannie stared at her sister. "Ok, fine. It hurt a little the first time I saw Emmie and Charlie run to Barbara instead of me, but that was momentary. Overall, I am delighted to have them, and by far, I am more pleased that those children have even more love in their lives than any smidgeon of hurt feelings. Besides, I know it's silly and selfish to feel that way."

"Knowing it in your head and feeling it in your heart are two different things," said Bonnie.

"Yes, but one thing you know about me, Bonnie, I will never let my feelings deter me from doing what's right."

The rest of the group started to filter in the front door having completed the unloading of the Cannady's moving truck.

"Ma, I'm home, and I'm hungry!" yelled Michael from the living room.

"Well, this conversation is over," said Bonnie to Jeannie.

"Absolutely," said Jeannie.

Chapter Twelve

Elizabeth loved her morning phone calls with her fiancé. Waking up to hearing his voice was one of the things she treasured in her day.

"I'm telling you, Rick," she said, "I've gone through a lot of moves with my family – and with my friends, but there is no one I know that fretted about every little thing the way Barbara did. It didn't matter if we unloaded a table or a doily, she was a nervous wreck."

Rick sipped his freshly squeezed juice. "I noticed. I was so glad to be with the guys unloading the truck. I didn't have to deal with all the chatting about where the little stuff went; only the big items."

"You got to leave early, too," said Elizabeth.

Rick laughed. "Yes, I got the privilege of leaving the moving and coming to work."

"True," said Elizabeth, "but where would you rather have been?"

"At work."

"I thought so," said Elizabeth.

"Did it get any better later in the day?" asked Rick.

"No, believe it or not, she seemed even more stressed out later at my folks' house, though she said she was 'calming down.' She drove poor Myrtle nuts with her endless questions about the house."

"I'm surprised Myrtle didn't say something to her," said Rick. "We all know she isn't one to mince words."

Elizabeth began making her bed as she continued to talk to him.

"Thankfully, the conversation eventually morphed into something else," she said. "You know how our family conversations go."

"Yes, I do," said Rick. "I don't get to attend many of the Sunday night dinners with my work schedule, but I've heard enough of them on other occasions to know the pattern."

He took a large sip of the juice, consuming the last of it.

"What else came up last night?" he asked.

"Well, let's see," said Elizabeth. "Angela is taking yet another knitting class over at the yarn shop. Uncle Deke and Michael are hard at work closing down the campground and readying it for winter. Oh, and as yet, nobody has heard from anyone they know about the candlesticks."

"I have my dad putting out some feelers to my side of the family as well," said Rick, "but so far, no word."

Elizabeth smoothed the spread on her bed and began putting on the decorative pillows. She heard a rumbling sound coming from the direction of Main Street. She looked at the clock.

"I think the school bus just went by," said Elizabeth. "I guess I'd better go."

"I love you," said Rick.

"I love you, too," said Elizabeth. "It's so nice to know that all our living plans and wedding plans are pretty much done – at least for the moment, and that there is no more tension in our lives about any of it. What a blessing!"

"Stephanie's parents are moved into Myrtle's old house. Your Uncle Deke is drafting some renovation plans for us, and the wedding is on the horizon," said Rick. "All is well."

Chapter Thirteen

The Yarkton House dining room table was strewn with cards, stamps, return address labels, and Elizabeth's address book. Rick and Elizabeth each grabbed a card from the pile and began to write.

"How many more lunch hours do you think it's going to take to finish these thank you notes?" asked Rick.

"It's only been yesterday and today that we've worked on these," said Elizabeth.

"I know," said Rick.

"And, I spent last night working on a bunch of these as well," said Elizabeth.

Rick thumbed through the stack. "I thought this pile had gone down a lot. That was part of my question. I didn't know how we did so many in one lunch hour."

"That's because we didn't do them all in a lunch hour," said Elizabeth. "Add about three hours of last night for me."

"I'm sorry, Bets," said Rick.

"For what?" asked Elizabeth.

"That I can't be here at night to help you," said Rick. "A lot of husbands work eight to five."

"So?" said Elizabeth.

"Well, you work mainly days, unless something comes up with one of your patients or the bed and breakfast," said Rick. "I work mostly nights and on weekends. That doesn't leave us a lot of 'couple' time."

Elizabeth thought for a moment. "Look at it this way, Rick.

Our children will never have to wonder if one of us will be able to come to their school functions because one of us will always be available."

"You're a smart woman," said Rick. "Do you know that?"

"I must be," said Elizabeth. "I fell in love with you."

They continued to write, sometimes one asking the other for suggestions on how to word something. They wanted their messages to be individual and reflect how much they appreciated what each guest, or gift-sender, had done for them.

"Hey," said Rick, "it's after one. Won't you be late for your next patient?"

"I'm good," said Elizabeth. "My next appointment isn't until two. Bridget will call me when they're here."

They finished around quarter-to-two.

"All done," said Rick. "Hallelujah."

"The only thing missing is to thank the people that gave us the candlesticks," said Elizabeth.

"I'm running out of options here," said Rick. "I do have feelers out to the family, but there are so many in the group, that unless we're lucky, we won't find out until the wedding."

"It's still a possibility that we won't ever know," said Elizabeth. "I hate to have someone out there who thinks we don't care enough to send a thank you."

"That is a possibility," said Rick. "I guess we could put a note on the center table at the wedding reception saying that to let us know if they were the sender."

Elizabeth sighed. "I'll keep asking around, too, just in case it wasn't someone from your family. My mom has been talking to some of our extended family as well. It's touchy, though. You don't want people to think we're looking for more presents. Yet, we don't want someone to feel unappreciated." She sighed again. "I'm not sure what else to do."

"Short of taking out ads in every newspaper where we have relatives, I don't think there is anything else we *can* do," said Rick.

They were silent for a bit when Rick let out a short laugh.

"What's funny?" asked Elizabeth.

"I'm picturing how my family is going to respond when they find out there was no card with the package," said Rick.

"Mad?" asked Elizabeth.

"Somebody's head will roll," said Rick. "At the very least, they will hear about it for the rest of their lives."

"I kind of feel sorry for her – or him," said Elizabeth.

She looked at the candlesticks, which now graced the dining room table. "They sure are beautiful, though," she said.

Chapter Fourteen

It had been an exhausting, twelve-plus hour day at the veterinary clinic. In addition to the animals who were ill, many of Elizabeth's appointments were filled with routine physicals, nail clips, and grooming. By the end of it all, both Elizabeth and Bridget flopped into chairs in the living room and put their feet up on the hassocks.

"I don't know about you," said Bridget, "but I opt for asking Rick to have a pizza delivered here tonight. I am exhausted."

Elizabeth closed her eyes for a second. "I don't even feel like eating. I could go straight to bed."

"Me, too," said Bridget, "but you and I both know that's not a good idea. I've at least had a quick lunch and a snack, but I don't think you've eaten since breakfast."

"I haven't," said Elizabeth. Her stomach growled. She opened her eyes and said, "Ok, pizza it is."

She gave Rick a quick call to place the order.

"Bridget," said Elizabeth, "I want to tell you how much our friendship means to me."

"Thank you," said Bridget. "I feel the same about you. You're a good friend and a good boss."

"Thanks," said Elizabeth. "Sometimes I feel like you really run the clinic, and I just take care of the patients."

Bridget brushed her hair back from her face. "Isn't that what you are supposed to do, Dr. Anderson?"

"Haha," said Elizabeth. "Yes, but you handle almost everything else in there. From greeting people, to scheduling appointments, to taking payments, to – well, pretty much all of it."

"I love it, and you know it," said Bridget.

"Yes, and you help me with the bed and breakfast, too," said Elizabeth.

"Not much," said Bridget. "I'm here on Sunday mornings to do some dishes. Big deal."

"It is to me," said Elizabeth. "Plus, you fill in when I'm not here."

"That's rare," said Bridget. "Elizabeth, you hardly ever take a day off."

"I'm taking over a week to go on my honeymoon," said Elizabeth.

"I would hope so," said Bridget. "Other people might want to honeymoon here at Yarkton House, but I don't think it would be good for you to do that. A change of environment is good for newlyweds."

Elizabeth smiled. "Yes, I love my home, and I love Pineville, but sometimes I like getting away. Being with Rick is going to be so wonderful."

"I'm sure it will be," said Bridget. "I know people don't send a lot of postcards anymore, but could you buy one or two for me or send me a few pictures by email? I love to see the world, and the farthest I got this summer was Milwaukee."

"Plan a vacation sometime after we get back, Bridget," said Elizabeth. "You don't have to wait until next year."

"Thanks, I appreciate that," said Bridget, "but I am saving to go to Ireland and see the area where my dad's side of the family originated."

"At least take a few days and go visit the friends in Madison or something," said Elizabeth. "You're here almost as much as I am."

"We can talk about that when you get back," said Bridget.

"I cannot believe how many people decided to bring their pets in for nail clips and things this week," said Elizabeth.

"I can," said Bridget. "It's your last day in the clinic until after your honeymoon. They all want to get ahead of the schedule rather than behind it. I'm guessing they're also wondering how booked you will be upon your return."

"I don't know that we'll have anything routine for a while when I get back," said Elizabeth. "They're all doing it now. We might be really slow."

"Dare to dream, Elizabeth," said Bridget.

Chapter Fifteen

She sat at one of the small tables in her aunt's bakery and worked on some of the details for her wedding. She nibbled on a cranberry orange scone and sipped a cup of coffee.

"Are you hiding out or something today?" asked Aunt Bonnie.

"No, why?" asked Elizabeth.

"Don't get me wrong, I'm glad you're here," said Bonnie, "but with all the space you have at Yarkton House, plus you can always sit at Rick's, I'm surprised you chose my place to work on this."

"I wanted a space to clear my head," said Elizabeth. "I'm stuck on the last couple of pieces for the ceremony, and I thought maybe a change of scenery would help."

"Is it?" asked Bonnie.

"Sort of," said Elizabeth. "The scone is definitely putting my head in a happier place than the tuna sandwich I ate for lunch."

"That is one of the wonderful things about working in a bakery," said Bonnie. "It's hard to be in a bad mood when you are surrounded by this much sugar and spice and the tantalizing smells that go with them." She took a deep breath. "I think the smells are why I became a baker."

"I will say it's one of the benefits of being your niece," said Elizabeth. "I know you'll always having something in the bakery that can make me smile."

"You know, a lot of brides turn over all of the ceremony details to the minister," said her aunt. "They tend to focus more on the reception."

"I want to focus on both," said Elizabeth. "Pastor Plain will do a lovely ceremony. I know that, and I am not trying to do anything that would infringe on his message or the way he handles weddings. My focus is on my vows to Rick and making each of these Bible verses match the person who is reading them."

"What about the music?" asked Bonnie.

"Dad and I figured that out a long time ago," said Elizabeth. "It does help when your dad is the organist at the church."

"Almost as good as having an aunt who is a baker?" asked Bonnie.

"Almost," said Elizabeth with a smile.

"How about the flowers?" asked Bonnie. "Do you have anything else to do with those before the big day?"

"Done."

"And the dresses?" asked her aunt.

"Just need to pick them up," said Elizabeth.

"Hair appointments arranged?" asked Bonnie.

"Of course," said Elizabeth.

"Sounds to me like you have everything well in hand," said her aunt.

Elizabeth looked down at her notes and the scattered sticky notes she had in her wedding notebook. "For the most part."

Chapter Sixteen

The slow, rhythmic kneading of Rick's hands on Elizabeth shoulders helped her relax. "Mmmm," she sighed.

"Feeling better?" he asked.

"Much," she said.

"Where else hurts?" asked Rick.

"Just a little lower in my shoulder blades," she said.

His hands moved down a few inches. "Here?" he asked.

"Oh, yes," said Elizabeth.

Rick pressed his thumbs deeper into the knot that had formed in her lower shoulder area. "Let me know if this pressure is too much," he said.

"Mm, no, not at all," said Elizabeth. "It feels good. I've been walking around like a human question mark these past few days. I can't seem to even stand up completely straight. I feel constantly hunched over."

Rick gently pulled the tops of her shoulders backward. "You are slumped forward, Bets," he said. "What have you been doing?"

"Probably too much of everything," said Elizabeth. "Writing all those notes, running errands, doing some last-minute planning and cleaning before our wedding, and a whole lot of other things."

"It feels like it," said Rick. "Usually, your shoulders are soft. Today, they feel like rocks."

"Why, do I feel a little less feminine?" asked Elizabeth.

Rick continued to massage her shoulders. "It has nothing

to do with your femininity. It has everything to do with your tension level."

"I know," said Elizabeth, "but when I think of tight muscles, I think of men, not women."

Rick paused for a second. "Which men would those be?"

Elizabeth giggled. "Only you, of course."

He started the massage once again. "Well, I'm not sure I believe that, but it sure sounds good."

"Sometimes I wish I was pizza dough," said Elizabeth.

"Because you would be with me more often?" he asked.

"That, too," she said, "but mainly because I'm jealous."

"Huh? Let me get this straight. You're jealous of pizza dough?"

"Definitely."

"That's going to need some explanation."

"You knead pizza dough for hours every day," said Elizabeth. "I've gotten about fifteen minutes of that this afternoon, and it's absolutely wonderful."

"Hm," said Rick, "maybe I should become a massage therapist instead of a cook."

"No way," said Elizabeth.

"As a second job then?" he asked.

"Not hardly," she said.

"Why not? We could always use the extra income," he said.

"Are you fishing for compliments?" she asked him.

"No."

"Then let's get at least one thing straight before the wedding day," she said.

"What's that?"

"The only shoulders you'll be massaging are mine," she said. "I will share you with pizza dough, but I am not sharing your hands with any other female. Are we clear on that, Mr. Polisari?"

He turned her to face him and gave her a long romantic kiss. "Crystal clear, Dr. Polisari."

"I'm not a 'Polisari' yet," said Elizabeth.

Rick leaned back on the couch and groaned. "I know. This

waiting is agonizing."

"One week from tomorrow, Rick," she said.

"Eight days too long," said Rick.

Chapter Seventeen

"Good grief!" said Stephanie as she walked from her car over to her best friend and sister-in-law, Julia. "The traffic on Main Street is ridiculous! I'm sure glad I didn't want to park over there. People are driving around the block waiting for spots to open."

Julia smiled. "You ready to head over to the Farmer's Market? I promised Lucas I would get back as soon as possible today so he can go work at the campground."

Stephanie nodded, and the two began to walk toward Roosevelt Park.

As Stephanie had said, cars were moving at a crawl down the busiest street in town. If any car exited a parking spot, the next person in line grabbed it.

"Wow. Traffic is heavy! It's a blessing to live where I do," Julia said. "One advantage is I never have to worry about downtown parking."

"Not with living a block off Main Street," said Stephanie. "You and Elizabeth have it made in that way. Speaking of Elizabeth, have you heard from her this morning?"

"Yes," said Julia, "she will meet us at the front of the park."

"Quick walk for her," said Stephanie. "It's even more convenient for her than it is for you. She's right across the street from it."

"The park is more convenient for Elizabeth. The church and school are more convenient for me," said Julia. "Everything else downtown falls somewhere in between."

"Your street will be full of cars later today," said Stephanie. "Once the school parking lot is full, you know your street is going to get people who are also headed to the parade or the game. I'm glad I don't need to drive over here then."

"That's right," said Julia. "You're not going to the parade or the game today, are you?"

"I might go to the parade," said Stephanie. "Emmie and Charlie will love it. Hopefully, Jackson and Jillian will stay calm in their stroller."

"If you do decide to go, Uncle Wilbur has once again said people can use the church parking lot," said Julia.

Stephanie shook her head. "I won't drive back," she said. "If I do come back later, it will be with Michael or Angela. I don't want to handle all four kids in a crowd by myself."

"I don't know when Lucas will get back from working today," said Julia. "Margaret and I will watch the parade from my porch. You're welcome there as well, you know."

"Thanks," said Stephanie. "I think I will take you up on that. Emmie and Charlie can sit at the curb on a couple of folding chairs, and the twins and I will come sit with you. That's another advantage for you, Jules," said Stephanie. "Ring side seats for the homecoming parade."

Elizabeth was waving to them as they arrived at the corner in front of the park entrance. "Good morning!" she said.

"Do you think Main Street will see an open parking spot anytime at all today?" asked Stephanie.

"This day is packed from morning 'til night," said Elizabeth. "The last day of the Farmer's Market this morning, then we have the homecoming parade in the early evening. Then, it's right over to the high school football field for the big game. It's crazy!"

"The town loves it, though," said Julia.

"You know," said Stephanie, "Joseph told me that some years ago, the town council thought about voting to end the Farmer's Market one week earlier, but the residents didn't want them to do that. So, they must like the chaos of this day."

"I think that was when I was in Madison," said Elizabeth. "I only have a vague recollection of that."

"Lucas told me about that meeting, too," said Julia. "He said people told them flat out to leave their tradition alone."

"Tradition?" asked Stephanie.

"Yes," said Julia, "the first Saturday in October is homecoming weekend and the market's last day. I guess people see it as a marker of some sort."

"When we were kids," said Elizabeth, "we always thought it moved the season."

"What?" asked Stephanie.

"Well," said Elizabeth, "it went from daily routine to thinking about the upcoming holidays."

"Thanksgiving and Christmas are months later," said Stephanie.

"Ah, but there's Halloween, too," said Elizabeth. "You know how excited kids get about Trick or Treat and Halloween parties."

"Oh, yes," said Stephanie. "I teach kindergarten, remember? And you're right. Once October comes, the kids start talking about their costumes and wanting to color pumpkins. It's really quite a fun time for them."

"For teenagers, there's also the haunted house things," said Elizabeth. "Plus, we have that huge Harvest Dance."

"Oh, that dance is so much fun!" said Stephanie.

"I guess it all makes sense when you think about it," said Julia. "One big day with homecoming and the market's finale for the year, then move on to the other fun stuff. It has a certain feel of 'joy to come' to it."

"Maybe that's why the campground closes this weekend as well," said Stephanie.

"You're on the right track," said Elizabeth. "Summer is definitely over. The camping numbers go down dramatically after Labor Day weekend. The people who come in September are looking for a different feel. They want a slower pace. Most are either fishermen or people who really want total peace and quiet."

They walked down the aisles, stopping at many of the vendors' tables. Throughout the summer, many of the merchants remained the same. The townspeople who frequented the market often came to know many by name.

Elizabeth, Julia, and Stephanie stocked up on many of their favorite market items. Although each of them had other things to do that day, no one hurried. It was a bittersweet time. The market wouldn't reopen until May, and that was the better part of another year.

No one felt that more than Julia. Her eyes took on a pensive look as she stared out in the distance at the line of stalls.

"You ok, Jules?" asked Stephanie.

"Every summer, I come here almost every Saturday morning," said Julia. "I love it so much."

"I know," said Stephanie.

"It just seems as though something is missing from my week when I'm not here," Julia said.

"We can't wait to see you next week!" yelled a couple of women as they passed Elizabeth.

Julia's mood brightened. "It's a good thing you're getting married next Saturday, Elizabeth! I won't have time to think about missing the first week with no Farmer's Market!"

"That's why we planned it that way!" said Elizabeth.

Julia started to laugh. "Thank you," she said. "This is what I needed today; a great time with you two."

"What a crazy few months this has been!" said Stephanie. "First, there was the whole 'Myrtle and Deke' thing. Then, my parents bought Myrtle's house. Michael's dated half the women in the state of Wisconsin. The twins and Margaret are all walking and getting into things left and right. Last week was your wedding shower, and next week is your wedding! We started with Uncle Deke's wedding, and we'll end it with yours."

"Two weddings in the family again this year," said Elizabeth. "We just had that a couple of years ago with the two of you. At least this time, the family will have had a few months in between."

"I think Don and Jeannie are still reeling from Deke marrying Myrtle," said Stephanie. "You and Rick? Well, for that I think they would say it's about time."

Elizabeth laughed at her. "You sure call things as you see them, don't you, Stephanie?"

"I sure do," Stephanie said. "I think it's one of the things your brother loves most about me. He never has to worry about how I'm feeling because I tell him."

"*Now* you do," said Julia.

"What's that supposed to mean?" said Stephanie.

"Steph," said Julia, "you know you've been my best friend since forever, but I remember a time when you hid your true feelings about Joseph."

"You're talking about before we were dating," said Stephanie.

"And a few times when you were," said Julia. "Remember when he had that horrible fall?"

"That was one of the scariest moments of my life," said Stephanie.

"We were all scared when that happened," said Elizabeth.

"I think it forced you to realize the depth of your feelings for him," said Julia.

"I knew how I felt about him long before that," said Stephanie. "I didn't want to jinx whatever we had."

"You didn't even know what you had," said Julia.

"You didn't know my brother loved you?" said Elizabeth.

"I wasn't sure," said Stephanie. "I knew I loved him, though."

"He's a dolt sometimes," said Elizabeth. "With Joseph, you have to be clear about how you feel and what you want from him. He's a lamebrain when it comes to figuring out women. He never had to. Tracy was in his life throughout school. They both simply 'knew' they were meant to be together."

"You and Rick are meant to be together, too," said Julia.

Elizabeth smiled. "Thank you."

She looked down at her cell phone. "Oh! Speaking of which, I promised him I would help him today at the restaurant. This is one of his busiest days of the year. Roxanna and I are both going to help him out."

"Honestly, both you and Roxanna are gluttons for punishment," said Stephanie.

"What?" asked Elizabeth.

"You work such long hours at the clinic and the bed and breakfast," said Stephanie. "You finally take a few days for yourself, and you're going over to wait tables at the pizza restaurant on homecoming night. That's not exactly resting up for your wedding."

"No, but I want to be there for Rick," said Elizabeth. "He's there for me. Always. Not to mention how he comes over every Sunday morning to help me with the bed and breakfast meals."

"I get it," said Stephanie. "I just marvel at how much you do."

"Roxanna is the one who marvels me," said Elizabeth. "Her art is exquisite. One look at her paintings, and you can tell how gifted she is. Yet, she helps at the diner a couple days a week, and at Rick's whenever he knows things will be busy."

She looked Stephanie in the eyes. "I mean, I love the man. He's there for me. We're a couple. However, Roxanna doesn't have that connection, not with Rick anyway. Yet, she is there."

"She's like Michael in that way," said Stephanie. "She's there for whomever needs her. Her art is her mainstay and her passion. Yet, she never fails to help a friend."

"Well," said Julia, "I am so happy that we are surrounded by caring people. I am also happy that there is so much love in this family; Lucas and me, Joseph and Steph, Deke and Myrtle, and now you and Rick. We are so blessed!"

"As much as I am looking forward to my wedding," said Elizabeth, "I am also wanting to actually be married and not have this tension. Rick is sick of dating. I don't need to be entertained by him anymore but sitting on the couch watching a movie is getting old for me, too."

"I understand," said Julia. "Lucas and I were quite ready for the wedding. Dating is wonderful, but there is a time when you're ready to get on with life."

"I can't really add much to this conversation," said Stephanie.

"My engagement was short, and much like Deke's wedding to Myrtle, Joseph and I got married rather suddenly. I still liked dating him."

"Looking back," said Elizabeth, "would you rather you had waited for the Christmas wedding you were originally planning to have?"

"No," said Stephanie. "The best thing I ever did in my life was marry your brother."

"Seven more days," said Elizabeth.

"Go serve some pizza," said Stephanie, "and get your mind off it for a while. You're going to worry yourself sick counting the seconds on the clock and the dates on the calendar, plus any other thing that comes up between now and then. Don't worry, Elizabeth. Rick's a great guy. He's anxious to be your husband. You're anxious to be his wife. What else matters?"

Chapter Eighteen

When Elizabeth arrived at Rick's Pizza, food prep for the busy day was already in full swing. Rick's dad was in the restaurant kitchen washing and chopping vegetables while Rick hauled out the heavy bags and cans necessary to get ready for the oncoming rush.

"Hello!" said Elizabeth. She walked in the kitchen and gave Rick's dad a peck on the cheek. "You guys are at it early!"

"Busy day," said Rick, Sr. "Glad you are here. We need extra hands on days like today, but he's stubborn, this one. Doesn't like to ask for help."

With four, ten-pound cans of tomato sauce in his arms, Rick stopped and stared at Elizabeth, waiting to hear how she would answer his father.

"Yes, I hear he can be that way," she said.

"You should talk," said Rick.

Rick's dad looked at Elizabeth as well. "I hear you do the same thing. Push yourself too hard. That's not good for you. The two of you will have to learn. It's good to work hard. Not good to work until you are stressed and too tired. I don't want to see either one of you do that to yourselves. It makes terrible problems."

"You don't need to worry about us," said Elizabeth. "We're young yet. We can handle it."

"Young doesn't mean smart," said Rick's dad.

Roxanna and a couple of other staff members came in the front door.

"Papa Polisari!" said Roxanna. She came into the kitchen to greet him with a kiss on the cheek, too. "I didn't know if you would be here today or not. I'm so glad you are!"

Elizabeth and Roxanna worked together as they washed, dried, and set all the tables in the dining area.

"I can't believe you called Rick's dad, 'Papa Polisari,'" said Elizabeth.

"It fits him, don't you think?" said Roxanna.

"I guess it does," said Elizabeth, "but how did that start?"

"Oh, it's a long story," said Roxanna.

Elizabeth looked around the restaurant at all the tables yet to be cleaned and set. "About a dozen or so tables' worth would you say?"

Roxanna laughed. "Yeah, about that."

"So, give," said Elizabeth, "how did you come to call Ricardo Salvatore Polisari, Sr., 'Papa Polisari?'"

Roxanna handed Elizabeth the drying towel and picked up the dish cloth. "It really goes all the way back to the first time I helped out here."

"Ok," said Elizabeth.

"I said to him, 'nice to meet you, Mr. Polisari,'" said Roxanna.
"Yes."

"Well, he looked at me and said, 'you're a grown-up woman, not a child. You can call me Rick,'" said Roxanna.

"I'm with you so far," said Elizabeth.

"I told him that I call his son, Rick, and that I thought it would be confusing if I called them both the same thing," said Roxanna.

"That's happened over the years," said Elizabeth. "Someone in the restaurant calls out, 'Rick,' and both of them turn around."

"Anyway," said Roxanna, "about that time, some kid in the restaurant saw his grandfather come in the door and yelled out, 'Papa!' I turned to Rick Sr. and jokingly said, 'I could call you Papa.'"

"That's it?" asked Elizabeth. "That's the whole story? You could have told me that while we were pouring sodas."

"It's the original story," said Roxanna, "but it's not the whole one."

Elizabeth tipped her head in a quizzical movement. "What's the rest of it?"

"You know, Rick's dad is really a sweet man," said Roxanna.

"He always has been," said Elizabeth.

"Often when I come here, it's because Rick knows it's going to be a busy day. You know, Valentine's Day, Father's Day, Homecoming."

"Yes."

"Well, when Rick knows ahead of time that it's going to be busy, his dad is often here," said Roxanna.

"His semi-retirement is only valid if the restaurant isn't swamped," said Elizabeth. "Even if he hears noise from here upstairs in his apartment, he will come down to check to see if Rick needs help."

"That figures," said Roxanna. "He is a quintessential 'father.' He would do anything for Rick and for many other people in his family, too."

"Ah, I get it," said Elizabeth, "a good father. Papa."

"There's even more to it than that," said Roxanna.

"Wow," said Elizabeth. "I guess it is a long story."

"You know," said Roxanna, "Rick hires a fair amount of high school and college kids to work here."

"Yes," said Elizabeth. "My parents do, also."

"Well, the kids either need to leave as soon as they can for homework and such, or they plain want to leave to go have fun with their friends," said Roxanna.

"No doubt about that," said Elizabeth.

"Often, when I'm here, it's the two Ricks and me who are left for the clean-up," said Roxanna. "Sometimes, Rick worries that his dad is doing too much and will ask me to get him to sit down for a while."

Elizabeth smiled. "Like father, like son. I can picture him doing that."

"However, he won't sit if I don't," said Roxanna. "I think it's a point of pride. The upshot is that we would start talking. Over the past year or so, those talks have gotten to a deeper level."

"He's a good man," said Elizabeth. "He would never betray a confidence."

"I know," said Roxanna. "You see, Elizabeth, I'm not very close with my own father. I never had heart-to-heart chats with him. He was a hard worker but didn't really have any close relationships with his daughters. These kinds of talks, well, they simply didn't occur. They mean a lot to me. Now, Mr. Polisari seems like Papa. It isn't a joke. It's how I really feel about him."

"Wow," said Elizabeth, "does Rick know this?"

"Which Rick?" asked Roxanna.

"I meant my Rick, but how about either of them," said Elizabeth.

"Your Rick, I don't know," said Roxanna. "I think maybe he thinks I still do it to get his dad to take a break. Papa P? Well, we've never talked about it, but I think he has much of it figured out."

"Roxanna," said Elizabeth, "I know you are closer to Stephanie than you are to me, but I sure wish we would spend more time together. You are an amazing person."

"Thank you," said Roxanna. "You know, when we were all kids hanging out at the campground in the summer, we all just played together. Once the summers ended, we didn't see each other until the following year. We camping kids were always envious of you Anderson kids."

"Really? Why?" asked Elizabeth.

"We thought you got to live like that all year," said Roxanna.

"To a point," said Elizabeth, "but once the season was over, we became regular school kids just as I assume you guys did."

"Elizabeth, let me tell you something," said Roxanna. "Yes, I know you went to college, vet school, and all that. However, for the most part, your whole life you lived here with all this natural beauty around you. No graffiti under the bridge or on buildings. No gang symbols. No real worries about violence. You have a world few people have."

"Yes, but we're still real people with real problems," said

Elizabeth.

"I'm sure you are," said Roxanna, "but I've got to tell you that on an average basis, the people in this town rank higher than almost any place I've lived or been. You have kindness. You have caring. And you? Elizabeth, you have one of the finest young men in this town wanting to marry you. I hope, truly hope, you know how lucky you are."

The before-parade crowd morphed into the after-parade crowd which corresponded with the pre-game crowd. The staff at Rick's did not need to look at their watches to know what time it was.

"My feet are killing me," said Elizabeth. She picked up an order from the silver serving shelf. "You think I would be used to this. I stand most of the day at the clinic."

"However, you also periodically sit," said Rick. "When was the last time you took a break?"

"I've been busy," said Elizabeth. "I haven't even thought about it."

"Well, think about it now, and go sit down," said Rick.

"Rick, every table in this place is filled," said Elizabeth. "I can't just walk off the floor. That would put more work on the rest of your staff."

"Yes, you can," said Rick. "I have plenty of help today. Just let them know, and they'll cover your tables. Each and every one of my waitstaff will pitch in to help. They're grateful to have some extra hands for whenever they're available."

"Thanks, I'll sit soon," said Elizabeth.

"Sit now," said Rick.

"Soon," said Elizabeth. "You have one of my orders ready right here on the shelf."

She gave him a smile and picked up a large deluxe pizza with double pepperoni. Continuing to smile at him and the customers, she headed for a group of teenagers.

Off and on during the afternoon and evening, Elizabeth

spotted some woman patron smiling or staring at Rick. One or two of them looked as though they would rather have Rick for supper than the garlic bread. With each time it happened, Elizabeth grew more annoyed by it.

It was getting near closing time when she saw it again. This time, there were two young women at a table in the center of the restaurant, both staring at her fiancé and whispering to each other. *Good grief,* she thought, *have these women any idea how ridiculous they look?*

The table was in her section. Swallowing her gnawing irritation, she went up to the table. She put on her best waitress smile. "Welcome to Rick's Pizza. How may I help you this evening?" she said.

"You could get us his phone number," said one of the women as she pointed at Rick.

Elizabeth's eyes grew wide.

Roxanna had passed the table as the words were spoken. She turned on her heel and grabbed Elizabeth by the arm. "Oh, Elizabeth," Roxanna said, "I'm so sorry I'm late getting here. I've got this but thank you for taking my table and helping these ladies."

"But it's my-" said Elizabeth.

"I know, it's your pleasure to be there for these ladies," said Roxanna, "but seriously, I've got it. I think table 13 wants some water."

Elizabeth was steaming as she walked away.

She went on with her work.

As they were closing that evening, Elizabeth spoke to Roxanna. "I don't know if I should thank you or yell at you for taking those two – um, women."

"You looked like you were going to rip their heads off," said Roxanna. "Besides, I heard that comment she made. If it were my fiancé, I might have been unhappy about it as well."

"Thanks," said Elizabeth. "It's ridiculous. I know we have a lot of out-of-towners here tonight with the homecoming game, but that was like watching a side show."

Roxanna tapped her shoulder. "The joys of dating the handsome."

Rick motioned for Roxanna to come and get his father.

"Papa Polisari," she called. "I'm dead on my feet and want to have a soda before I leave. Can you join me?"

"I don't want to leave all this cleaning for Rick," said his dad.

"Don't worry about it, Dad," said Rick. "I've got it. Roxanna wants to sit and talk. Can you take a soda out there?"

"I'll take two," said Rick, Sr.

He walked past Elizabeth. "Betsy, you come sit with us. You were working hard."

"Maybe in a little bit," said Elizabeth. "I want to talk to Rick for a minute."

She went into the kitchen where Rick was cleaning the workspace.

She followed behind him with a towel, drying what he had washed. "How often does this happen, Rick?"

"I have to clean and disinfect every night," said Rick. "You know the health codes for eating establishments."

"I'm not talking about health codes," said Elizabeth.

"Then, what are you talking about? How busy we were? I get probably a half-dozen days like this per year. Homecoming day is in the top three for income every year," he said.

"That's great," said Elizabeth, "but that's not what I mean, either."

Rick stopped cleaning and looked at her. "Bets, I need you to be more specific. I have had a busy day, and I'm probably not thinking as clearly as I should. Help me out here."

"I have been helping you out all day," said Elizabeth.

"I didn't mean it that way," said Rick.

"I know, but I just wanted to refresh your memory," said Elizabeth.

"Honey, you are in a sour mood," said Rick. "Go sit with my dad and Roxanna. I'll get you home as soon as possible."

"How many women, Rick?" asked Elizabeth.

Rick turned and faced her. "What on earth are you talking

about?”

“I want to know how many women throw themselves at you,” said Elizabeth.

“What women?” asked Rick.

“Oh, come on!” said Elizabeth. She struggled to keep her voice low so that Roxanna and Rick’s dad would not hear her. “I lost count today after six. I want to know how many women you have flirt or stare at you on a daily basis.”

“None,” said Rick.

“That’s not true,” said Elizabeth.

“Honey, on a daily basis, I have mostly local people in here. They all know me, and they all know you. Even more than that, they know we’re together. They’re not likely to start flirting with me even if they did find me appealing in some way.”

He looked at her face, which still held a grimace. “Besides, what’s so appealing about sweat and cheese?”

“Don’t play naïve with me,” said Elizabeth. “You know how you come across to women. A couple of them actually left their business cards on the table. One woman asked me if you would give her your ‘secret recipe,’ and she wasn’t referring to your minestrone. I thought those last two were going to throw you their house keys.”

“Did you see me look back at any of them?” asked Rick.

“No,” said Elizabeth.

“Then, what’s your concern?” asked Rick.

“Are you serious?” asked Elizabeth. “I hate seeing them look at you that way!”

“I can’t help for the way anyone looks at me,” said Rick. “I no longer encourage anyone who does.”

“But you did? Is that what you’re telling me?” asked Elizabeth.

“When we weren’t dating, yes, sometimes I did,” said Rick.

“Great,” said Elizabeth.

“Look, do you want me to lie to you?” asked Rick. “You know, those were six long years that you were gone. I didn’t run out to find someone, but I’m not going to lie and say I became a monk during that time."

"So, you *do* know how they look at you!" said Elizabeth.

"A lot of men look at you that way, too, Bets," said Rick.

"Not the same."

"Fine, who cares," said Rick. "You have me. I have you. We're getting married in a week. I don't care if they leave business cards or anything else. End of story. Ok?"

"I'm sorry, Rick. I'm on edge lately. I don't know why," said Elizabeth.

"You're tired, Bets," said Rick. "I'll take you home. My dad will lock up."

Chapter Nineteen

Bridget saw the living room lights from the top of the staircase. She knew from having looked at her clock as she awoke that it was still a little before four a.m. She softly walked down the first few steps and peered her head down into the living room.

Elizabeth sat rock still, feet propped on the couch, staring out at nothing. She was immersed in perplexing thoughts.

Bridget slowly walked over to her. It took Elizabeth a few moments to realize that Bridget was standing in the same room as she was sitting.

The break in her concentration startled her. "Oh!" Her body inadvertently shook.

"I didn't mean to frighten you," said Bridget. "I'm just wondering what you're doing. It's the middle of the night. Aren't your days long enough for you?"

Elizabeth let out a long sigh. "Too long sometimes."

"Then what are you doing here in the middle of the night?" Bridget asked.

"I'm so on edge, Bridget," said Elizabeth, "and I don't understand it."

"So, you think sitting in the living room with all the lights on at three-something in the morning is going to make that better?" Bridget asked.

"I don't know," said Elizabeth. "It can't make it worse."

Bridget stared down at her for a second. "Are you sure about that?"

Elizabeth tilted her head up. "What do you mean?"

"One of your biggest problems is that you often don't get enough sleep," said Bridget. "Yet, here you sit, lights blazing, when you could be upstairs sleeping."

"The problem is I wasn't sleeping," said Elizabeth. "I got sick of pacing around that one room."

"You want some company?" asked Bridget.

"Go back to bed," said Elizabeth. "There's no need for two of us to be without sleep."

Bridget motioned for Elizabeth to move her feet so she could also sit on the sofa. "So, what's up?"

"I snapped at Rick tonight," said Elizabeth.

"Why?" asked Bridget.

"Bridget, these women flirt with him!" Elizabeth said.

"Ok," said Bridget.

"No, it's not ok!" said Elizabeth.

Bridget backed up a few inches. "You're a wee bit sensitive."

"It made me sick to my stomach," said Elizabeth. "These women were so open about it! And there were quite a few that stared at him like he was the main course of the meal. It was disgusting."

"It was normal," said Bridget.

"How can you even say that?" said Elizabeth.

Bridget stared into Elizabeth's face before she replied. "Do you find Rick attractive?" she asked.

"Well, of course, I do," said Elizabeth.

"They do, too," said Bridget.

"But he's my fiancé," said Elizabeth, "not theirs."

"True," said Bridget. "Did you find him attractive before he was your fiancé?"

"Yes," said Elizabeth.

"Did you think that was in some way abnormal?" asked Bridget.

"Well, no, of course not," said Elizabeth. "First of all, I was in high school. Second, I didn't act ridiculous. Those women were so obvious, and some of them were outright offensive."

"Offensive to whom?" asked Bridget.

"Me," said Elizabeth.

"Were they staring at you?" asked Bridget.

"No, I told you. They were staring at Rick," said Elizabeth.

"Was Rick bothered by it?" asked Bridget.

"He said he didn't notice, nor did he care," said Elizabeth.

"Then why are you sitting here stewing about it?" asked Bridget.

"It's irritating," said Elizabeth.

Bridget shook her head. "Elizabeth, if you are going to be in love with a handsome man, you are going to have to get used to the fact that other people will see that, too. Short of having him make pizza in a muumuu and a mask, people are going to notice that he is extremely good-looking."

"A muumuu and a mask, huh?" said Elizabeth. "Maybe I should suggest he try that."

"You know people would still stare, right?" asked Bridget.

"Yes," said Elizabeth, "but then they would be staring at him because he looked odd, not gorgeous."

"And that's a better characteristic in a fiancé?" Bridget asked with her eyes wide in a definite questioning tone.

They both laughed softly so as not to wake the guests in the bed and breakfast rooms.

"Come on, Elizabeth," said Bridget, "let's get some sleep. We now have about an hour until those alarm clocks go off."

Chapter Twenty

There was much conversation and activity going on in Fellowship Hall that early October morning. Tables were full of parishioners talking about everything from their past weeks to politics. Children ran between the tables and off to the Sunday School rooms. Many people went through the doughnut and coffee line seeking out their morning favorites.

Elizabeth noticed none of it. She was standing next to the family table, no space between them, holding Rick's arm in a tight grip, and scanning the room.

He looked down at her. "Is something wrong?"

She looked up into his eyes. "No, why?"

"You've got my arm in a vise," said Rick.

She loosened her grip a bit but continued to hold it; nor did she move further away from his side.

"Are you cold?" he asked.

"No," said Elizabeth.

"Bets, not that I mind, because frankly I like having you close to me, but what is going on here?" asked Rick. "This," he struggled for the right word, "*closeness*, isn't like you. At least not when we're out in public."

"I'm not at all being inappropriate," said Elizabeth. "We're in church, for goodness' sake."

"I didn't say that," said Rick. "I said it was unlike you."

She smiled at him. "I think you should get used to it. I intend to keep myself well in sight of anyone who might have a fleeting notion that you were available."

An unreadable look flashed across his face. He led her away from the tables and into the vacant hallway. Once there, he took her arm from being entwined with his and put it at her side. He took one step away from her. "Is this still about last night? I told you. I no longer care. On a personal level, the only female that appeals to me is you."

"I know, but those women were so obvious! You couldn't help but notice!" said Elizabeth.

"I was busy. I was working. Even if I did, or would, notice, let me spell this out for you for the last, and I do mean last, time, Bets. I. Don't. Care."

She lowered her gaze. "I guess I believe you."

His eyes became a mix of hard and hurt. "You guess you believe me. Is that what you just said? It's six days until our wedding. You'd better decide by then whether you trust me or not. I love you. I've loved you for a long time, and you should know that. I have no intention of jeopardizing anything we've built."

He grimaced. "However, if you can't walk down that aisle with a full trust in me, please don't walk down it at all. I couldn't bear to be married to someone with those kinds of doubts."

He turned and walked up the steps. He needed some air.

Chapter Twenty-One

"I can't tell you the last time I was able to come to your bakery for breakfast, Bonnie," said Jeannie.

"Me, either," said Angela. She took a deep, exaggerated breath. "I forgot how good this place smells!"

Bonnie feigned sadness. "If you'd stop by more often, you wouldn't forget, Angela. Really, my own sister and niece don't even come to my business on a regular basis! I feel so ignored."

"When was the last time you were in the diner to eat?" Jeannie asked her sister.

"You know I work until mid-afternoon," said Bonnie.

"Well, you know we work during the day, too," said Jeannie.

"I know," said Bonnie. "I'm just giving you grief."

"Can I get a couple of your lemon macaroons to go, Aunt Bonnie?" asked Angela.

"Of course," said Bonnie. She put a few in a small, white bakery bag and came over to their table.

"Hey, I heard Elizabeth and Rick had some sort of row at the church yesterday," said Bonnie.

"It wasn't a row," said Jeannie.

"Well, I heard Rick left," said Bonnie.

"You seem to hear a lot of things," said Jeannie.

"Well," said Bonnie, "what happened? Nobody talked about it last night at dinner. I thought maybe we would. You know, to clear the air."

Jeannie set down her fork. "Bonnie, the only two that need to clear the air are Rick and Elizabeth, and Rick wasn't there. You know his restaurant is open on Sunday nights. He's never able to make the family dinners."

"All the more reason to say something," said Bonnie. "Elizabeth could have spoken openly about it."

"Obviously, she didn't want to do that," said Jeannie.

Bonnie looked at her niece. "Angela, did she say anything to you? You know, sisters tell each other a lot."

Angela looked at her mother.

"Sisters also keep confidences, Bonnie," said Jeannie.

"Hmmm, I suppose," said Bonnie. "Maybe she'll say something when she gets here."

"Bonnie, don't you dare bring it up," said Jeannie. "Judging from how quiet she's been about it, I don't think she wants to discuss it."

"Well, if she does bring it up, I'm asking," said Bonnie.

The bell above the bakery door tinkled.

"Ah, here comes the bride now!" said Bonnie.

"Good morning," said Elizabeth.

"Hi, Sweetheart," said her mother. "Do you want something to eat before we head out for the day?"

"No, thanks," said Elizabeth. "I had coffee before I left the house, and I don't think I want to eat any bakery before I try on my dress."

"You're not going to gain weight between here and the bridal salon," said Bonnie.

"It has to go somewhere if I eat it," said Elizabeth, "and I don't want it going anywhere that can expand my body before we make sure that dress fits."

"Coffee?" asked Bonnie.

"No, I would like to get going if you don't mind," said Elizabeth.

"Can I have five more minutes with my éclair?" asked Angela.

Elizabeth gave her a telling look.

"Oh," said Angela, "on the other hand, I am so full, I'd better not eat those last couple of bites."

"You know," said Bonnie, "if I didn't know better, I would

think you are trying to get away from me."

Elizabeth gave her a hug. "Now, Aunt Bonnie, why ever would you think something like that?"

They filled the car with chitchat about traffic, the weather, the family, and the colors of the autumn leaves. Even though they were heading to the bridal salon to pick up her wedding gown, very little was said about the wedding itself.

Once Elizabeth was in the dressing room with the clerk, and Jeannie and Angela were seated in chairs waiting for the bride to come out in her dress, Jeannie said, "Well, that was awkward."

"What do you mean, Mom?" said Angela. "We had a nice conversation in the car."

"I suppose you can call it nice," said Jeannie, "but someone on their way to get their wedding dress would usually throw in a comment or two about being excited about it."

"She's just lost in thought," said Angela.

"I also caught that exchange between the two of you at the bakery," said Jeannie. She put up her hand to stop her daughter from saying something she didn't want to hear. "And don't say 'what do you mean.' You know doggone well what I mean."

Angela looked uncomfortable.

"You don't have to tell me, Angela," said Jeannie. "If she doesn't want me to know, I will stay out of it."

"I don't think it's that at all," said Angela.

"She sure doesn't want Aunt Bonnie to know, because that means the whole town will know within two hours," said Angela.

"I know full-well my sister is a gossip," said Jeannie. "She may well be the queen of the Pineville branch."

"Elizabeth's business is her own," said Jeannie, "but I hope she's not building up emotions that don't have much bearing in reality. Elizabeth is not a gossip, but she does have a couple of tendencies that can hurt her."

"Like what?" asked Angela.

"Like her tendency to work too hard," said Jeannie, "and her tendency to work herself into a dither about something rather than coming right out and addressing it. The first is exhausting, both physically and mentally. The second is dangerous to long-term happiness."

Angela shuddered.

"I saw that," said her mother.

"Um, excuse me, Mrs. Anderson," said the salesclerk. "I think our bride is having some nervous jitters. I can't get her to stop crying. Perhaps it would be best if you came into the fitting room."

Chapter Twenty-Two

I f Elizabeth had been taking the lead on her morning phone call to Rick, the conversation would have been subdued at best, tear-laden at worst. Instead, Rick hardly noticed her semi-quiet, "Hello."

His voice was energized and full of enthusiasm. "Hey, guess who's coming into town today?"

"Well, as far as I know, nobody is due to come in for the wedding until tomorrow. Someone coming in for something with the restaurant?" she asked.

"Nope."

"Some politician visiting?" Elizabeth said. "No, wait, that can't be because Joseph would have told us."

"No, no politicians. No celebrities. No authors. No Broadway dancers."

"Ok, friend from school? Former Pineville resident?" Elizabeth asked.

"No."

"Then I'm fresh out of guesses," said Elizabeth. "Who is it?"

"Geno!" said Rick.

"I thought your cousin, Eugene, was coming in tomorrow," said Elizabeth.

"That was the original plan," said Rick. He began pulling all the ingredients for his fresh-squeezed juice from the refrigerator.

"What changed?" asked Elizabeth.

"He has quite a few vacation days in his account at work,"

said Rick. "He also said he saved fifty bucks on the flight."

"Does he want to move the pictures to a different date?" asked Elizabeth. "I arranged my hair and nail appointments based on the schedule he gave us."

"He doesn't want to change any of that," said Rick. "He said since he had all that vacation time coming, and he hadn't seen me in a number of years, that he would come in early. That way, we can hang out, just us, before the rest of the family arrives."

"That's thoughtful, I guess," said Elizabeth.

"What's the problem?" said Rick. "You don't sound too excited."

"It's not a problem. It's just unanticipated," said Elizabeth.

"That's true," said Rick, "I do have a couple of things to run past you given this latest surprise."

"Yes," said Elizabeth. Her tone was wary.

"I hope you don't get mad about this," said Rick.

"Well," said Elizabeth, "that's never a good opening."

"Normally, I wouldn't think twice about asking you, but given how the weekend went, I'm a little hesitant to ask," said Rick.

"About what?" said Elizabeth.

"Hang on a moment."

He made his morning juice. Carrots, ginger, cucumber, and a green apple whirred and spun their way through the machine. "Ok," he said, "I'm back."

"Did you have me hold so that you could make your morning juice, or so that you can formulate the right words to ask me whatever it is that you are going to?" said Elizabeth.

Rick chuckled. "Maybe a little bit of both."

"Ask me already," Elizabeth said. "I really don't want to think about this while you run for five miles."

"You know I always do my morning run before I call you," said Rick.

"Fine, quit stalling, please," said Elizabeth.

Rick took his first sip. "All right. He is getting into the Milwaukee airport around noon."

"How are you going to pick him up from MKE and get back here on time to open the restaurant? That's going to be tight," said Elizabeth.

"It will," said Rick. "My dad offered to go get him, but, Bets, I really don't want him to drive that far by himself," Rick said.

"I see," said Elizabeth. "So, you want me to drive with him to Milwaukee."

"If you wouldn't mind," said Rick.

"I can do that," said Elizabeth. "My next set of things to do for the wedding start tomorrow. By Thursday, things will get crazy as the bridal party and some of the family start to arrive. So, today is ok."

She looked at the clock on the table at her side. "You said he's coming in around noon?"

"Yes."

"When is your dad coming to pick me up?" asked Elizabeth.

"About fifteen minutes," said Rick.

"Rick!" said Elizabeth. "Why didn't you ask me this sooner?"

"He just changed his flight last night," said Rick.

"Spontaneous, isn't he," said Elizabeth.

Rick laughed. "That's an understatement."

"Ok," said Elizabeth, "before I hang up and throw myself together in record time, are there any other surprises you want me to know?"

"One," said Rick.

"And that is?"

"Eugene wants to spend some time with me tomorrow catching up on life and such," said Rick. "He's never been here without a whole bunch of family around. It would be nice to be able to do a few things with him."

"I agree," said Elizabeth. "What's the surprise?"

"Given how bothered you were by some of the out-of-town women at the restaurant, I want to make sure you are ok with him and me doing regular guy things without you being there," said Rick.

"What kind of 'guy' things?" asked Elizabeth.

"I thought I would take him fishing, maybe kayaking, and bowling," said Rick.

"No bars or dance clubs?" asked Elizabeth.

"Only if you want to call the bowling alley either of those," said Rick.

"Just go," said Elizabeth. "I understand you wanting to spend time with him. I'm not that kind of jealous. Good grief. Who would be jealous of a cousin?"

"I was more worried you would be jealous if we ran into any ladies while we were out," said Rick.

"I didn't even think of that until you said it!" said Elizabeth.

"Uh-oh," said Rick. "Did I open Pandora's box?"

"No, I'm fine," said Elizabeth.

She looked out her front window. "Oh, no!"

"What's the matter?" said Rick.

"Your dad's already here!"

Rick laughed. "Have a good day – and thanks for doing this for me."

"It's now only four more days until the wedding," said Elizabeth. "No more surprises, ok?"

"Ok."

"I'll talk to you later," said Elizabeth. "Do me a favor and let Sniffy out before you start work. Bridget is in Madison, and it will get pretty long for him to wait to go."

"Not a problem," said Rick. "Sniffy and I will be fine. That dog and I are buddies."

"I love you," said Elizabeth. "Never forget that."

"I love you, too," said Rick. "Enjoy Cousin Eugene. He's a hoot!"

"Keep your eyes open for Eugene," said Rick's dad.

"There are an awful lot of people out here," said Elizabeth. "How am I supposed to know which one he is? I've never seen him."

"Trust me," said Mr. Polisari. "You'll know."

They drove at a crawl past a number of cars, vans, shuttle buses, and people. On a couple of occasions, Elizabeth thought for a brief moment she had spotted him. Then, she did.

"He's right under that parking lot sign!" said Elizabeth.

Rick's dad pulled over as close to the curb as traffic would allow. "Roll down your window and call him."

"Eugene!" she said. "Over here!"

The man at the curb with the shocking red hair and the accordion case peered over at the car.

"It's Mr. Polisari and Elizabeth!" she said.

The man grabbed his case, his rolling bag, and a secondary bag. He struggled to get to the car.

"Oh, goodness," said Elizabeth. "That's a lot of stuff!"

"I probably forgot half of what I wanted to bring!" said Eugene. "I know I wanted to bring more lenses for my camera, but with baggage restrictions what they are, I decided to forego a few."

Rick's dad stepped out of the car and popped the trunk. "Eugene!" he said and gave him a hug. "Rick is sorry he couldn't be here to greet you."

"Zio Ricardo! I didn't expect you to drive all this way! I could have taken a bus," said Eugene.

"A bus to Pineville?" said Elizabeth.

"I guess I shouldn't have changed my flight," said Eugene.

"Don't be silly," said Rick's father. "Rick is looking forward to seeing you. Don't plan on sleeping late tomorrow, either. He wants to take you fishing."

"Don't the fish bite later in the day?" said Eugene.

"You don't fish much, do you?

"Of course," said Elizabeth.

"You know, Ric'O told me you were pretty, but I never expected you to be beauty queen gorgeous!" said Eugene.

Elizabeth remembered Rick telling her that Eugene would ply her with compliments. She smiled. "I think that's a bit of an overstatement, but thank you," she said.

"Overstatement? Oh, child, you are ravishing!" he said. He

put the bags in the trunk and climbed into the back seat.

Elizabeth started to say something, but Eugene put his finger up to stop her.

He dialed his cell phone. "Ric'O! I'm in the back seat of Zio's car, and we're on our way back to you. Why didn't you warn me this bride of yours was so breathtaking! My goodness. She must have every man from Chicago to Nantucket turning in her direction."

There was a bit of silence as Eugene listened to Rick's response.

"Hey, seriously, I am sorry if this change in plans made a mess of things," said Eugene.

He waited for another response.

"Ok," said Eugene, "I will see you soon. Can't wait to go fishing tomorrow. You better get up before the fish stop biting!"

He disconnected from the call. "Do you have some poor guy with allergy issues in your town?"

"It's fall in Wisconsin. That probably describes one third of the population," said Elizabeth. "Why?"

"He said he had to go take care of Sniffy," said Eugene.

Both Rick's dad and Elizabeth started to laugh.

"I love, love, love to laugh," said Eugene, "but why is that funny?"

"Because Sniffy is Elizabeth's dog," said Rick's dad.

Elizabeth was sitting in the Yarkton House living room when Bridget arrived home from her trip to Madison. She was smiling and humming to herself as she enjoyed the warmth and crackle of the fire in the grand old fireplace.

"Hey, Bridget!" Elizabeth said as her assistant and friend came in the front door. "How was Madison?"

"Um, ok," said Bridget. Her tone was wary.

"Didn't you have a good time?" asked Elizabeth.

"Um, I'm tired," said Bridget. "It's been a long day."

"Oh, I'm sorry," said Elizabeth. "Good night, then. We can

catch up in the morning. I have had such a fun day. I'm having a hard time winding down to sleep. However, this fireplace is certainly helping."

"I'm glad to see your mood has lightened," said Bridget. "What changed?"

"Rick's cousin, Eugene, is an absolute sweetheart!" said Elizabeth. "He kept me laughing all the way back from Milwaukee."

"I'm grateful for that," said Bridget. "You've been so stressed out lately. I was worried about you."

Elizabeth sat up straighter on the couch and motioned for Bridget to sit near the fire. "You know me," said Elizabeth. "I worry about things I really shouldn't."

Bridget's tone was noncommittal. "Yeah."

"Wow," said Elizabeth, "you really are tired. You sit and rest. I'll make you a cup of tea."

Bridget shook her head no. "You don't need to do that. I'll just head upstairs and go to bed." She stood up from the sofa.

Elizabeth waved her back. "Sit. You look dog tired, and that's not a vet pun, although I think Eugene would love it!"

"You're really fond of Rick's cousin, aren't you?" said Bridget.

"Yes, I am," said Elizabeth. "I swear that man could take the weight of the world off anyone's shoulders."

As Elizabeth headed into the kitchen to make the tea, Bridget said under her breath, "I hope so."

When Elizabeth came back with a steaming mug of herbal tea, she found her friend standing in front of the fireplace staring into it. She handed her the mug. "Did you have a bad ride home?"

"No," said Bridget. "It was fine."

"You seem as though you have something on your mind," said Elizabeth.

"I told you. I'm tired," said Bridget. "I'll go up to bed now."

Elizabeth touched her on the arm. "Wait a minute. Bridget, you and I know each other far too well for me to accept that. Something is definitely on your mind."

"Yeah," said Bridget, "but I don't want to talk about it right now."

"Why?"

"You've had a good day. You're happy. Let's leave it at that for now," said Bridget. "We'll talk tomorrow. I promise."

"Now, I'm going to spend half the night lying awake wondering what the heck happened," said Elizabeth. "Just tell me. We'll work it out together. I promise."

"You and I can't work this out," said Bridget.

"Bridget, what could be that bad that a friend can't help?" said Elizabeth.

"This is not about you and me," said Bridget.

"Ok," said Elizabeth, "but whatever happened, Bridget, I promise, I am here for you. We can talk it through."

Bridget sighed. Her mouth formed a grimace. "This isn't about me."

"All right," said Elizabeth, "if you are keeping a confidence for someone else, I respect that. I won't ask you anymore."

Bridget nodded and turned to leave the room. At the base of the stairs, she turned back to Elizabeth. "I know who gave you the candlesticks."

"Oh, wonderful!" said Elizabeth. "Who is it?"

"Randy."

Chapter Twenty-Three

"What am I going to do?! Oh, Bridget, why?" Elizabeth asked.

"First of all, breathe," said Bridget. She handed her the mug. "Here, I think you need this tea more than I do."

Elizabeth took a sip and handed the cup back to Bridget. "How long have you known this?"

"Just since today," said Bridget. "I spent most of the time since trying to figure out how I was going to tell you."

"And now, I have to figure out how to tell Rick!" said Elizabeth. She put her head in her hands and rubbed her temples. "Who did this? Why didn't she – or he – say something before now? How did Randy even know about the shower?"

"Whoa," said Bridget. She sat in a chair across from her friend and boss. "It's a long story."

"Well, I'm wide awake now," said Elizabeth. "Take as much time as you need, but please tell me what in the world happened!"

"Look, it was all very innocent on this person's part," said Bridget.

"Who was it?" asked Elizabeth.

Bridget shook her head no. "I don't want to tell you that until after the wedding."

"Why?" asked Elizabeth.

"Because I have a feeling you will either be angry or try to drill that person for more information," said Bridget.

"I am angry," said Elizabeth.

"Don't be," said Bridget.

"Easy for you to say," said Elizabeth. "You're not the one who has to tell your current fiancé that your former fiancé sent you a shower gift."

"You're making more out of this than needed," said Bridget.

"I'm afraid I don't think so," said Elizabeth.

"Tell me, Elizabeth," said Bridget, "are you angry with Randy, the person who delivered the gift, or are you just worried about Rick's reaction?"

"How about all three?" said Elizabeth.

"Let's examine that, shall we?" said Bridget.

"Why? Can't you simply accept that I am upset?" said Elizabeth.

"You used the word 'angry,'" said Bridget.

"I did, and I am," said Elizabeth.

"I'm not sure you are using the right word here," said Bridget, "at least not for all three."

Elizabeth let out an exasperated sound. "People don't think of how what they do affects others!"

"Sorry, Elizabeth," said Bridget, "but I disagree."

"How could you?" asked Elizabeth. "This was so heartless."

"You're wrong," said Bridget, "and you are only thinking with your raw, and spontaneous feelings right now."

"How else should I feel?" asked Elizabeth. "Things were just starting to get better after my stupidity last weekend. I was so angry that all those women were ogling Rick. I was so jealous!"

"That's not the subject at hand," said Bridget.

Elizabeth got up and started pacing around the living room. "Oh, that's where you are wrong, Bridget," said Elizabeth. I was so arrogant with him! I accused him of being a little too flattered by all that female attention, and when Rick said men look at me in that same way, I told him he was wrong. I negated everything he said. I was so immature and sure of myself. And now, I have to turn around and tell him that my old boyfriend/fiancé/ whatever you want to call him gave me an anonymous present.

Not to mention, he already knows it wasn't a cheap gift. So, let's add that to the mix."

"Elizabeth, just tell him the truth," said Bridget. "Rick loves you. It will be ok."

"Not initially," said Elizabeth.

"Maybe not," said Bridget, "but it will be. The biggest thing, as I see it, is that you don't make it into a long-drawn-out story. Tell him you heard that someone in Madison delivered the gift for Randy not realizing there wasn't a card inside. Once it became such a big question at the shower, she was afraid to say anything then."

"So, it's a woman that brought the gift?" asked Elizabeth.

"Yes, and the who really doesn't matter," said Bridget. "What does matter is that she really wasn't trying to hurt you, Rick, or the relationship between the two of you."

"Will you please tell me who it was?" asked Elizabeth.

"Not now," said Bridget. "I will after the wedding, if you still want to know. For now, I want to see you focus on the important things; being honest with Rick and knowing that Randy didn't ask her to deliver it to your shower. What he asked her was to give it to you prior to, or after the wedding, but not at the wedding itself."

"I don't know how I'm going to do this, Bridget," said Elizabeth.

"Think about it for the night. It will come to you," said Bridget.

They sat and talked for another hour. Once they had exhausted the conversation about the candlesticks, they moved on to other subjects. By the end of their talk, Elizabeth felt better.

Her cell phone buzzed. It was her answering service relaying a message about a horse that was a patient of hers.

After the call, Bridget said, "I thought you told the service you were on vacation."

"I left them a short list of exceptions," said Elizabeth. "However, even that stops as of Friday night."

"I would hope so," said Bridget.

"I'd better text Rick and let him know I won't be available for our morning call tomorrow," said Elizabeth.

"Oh?" said Bridget, "and why not?"

"I'm going out to see the horse," said Elizabeth. "I don't know when I'll get back. This could be a difficult delivery, and the family is quite worried about her."

"I can come along," said Bridget.

"I'll be ok," said Elizabeth. "After all, you're on vacation, too."

"So, what?" said Bridget. "You know, I am here for whatever you need."

"I need some answers," said Elizabeth.

"I'm afraid I can't give you those," said Bridget. "I can only give you my thoughts."

"Well," said Elizabeth, "hold that one. I'm going to grab my bag and get a quick text out to Rick for now."

She picked up her cell phone. *Rick, heading out of town to deliver a foal. I may get back quite late or even in the morning. Please have fun with Eugene tomorrow and tell him I send my love. I will catch up with you tomorrow night.*

Chapter Twenty-Four

October winds blew through the trees on the campground, and the water churned with the rhythm of the wind.

Rick and Eugene stood a few feet apart on the riverbank. Their lines were cast into the water. It had been the better part of a half-hour since a word had been spoken between the two of them.

"Ric'O," said Eugene, "I've heard that people like to be quiet when they fish, but is it mandatory? I feel like I'm meditating over here."

"Is that a bad thing?" asked Rick.

"Well, no," said Eugene, "but I usually do that sitting down. Standing on my feet staring at the water is putting me in a trance."

"I'm sorry," said Rick, "did you want to go?"

"No," said Eugene, "it's really quite beautiful here. However, I also want to have time to catch up with you. Once everyone gets here, I'll be lucky to catch you for five minutes in the hallway or something."

Rick smiled. "Geno, talk away. I haven't been this relaxed in months. It's rare I come out here."

"You live only a few miles from here. Plus, your fiancée's parents own the place," said Eugene.

"They don't own the river," said Rick, "but yes, all the rest is true."

"So, why aren't you here doing this more often?" asked

Eugene. "You said you enjoy it."

"I do," said Rick, "but with being engaged to Bets, my priorities have changed. Besides which, I have my restaurant, her B&B, and the wedding."

"She sure is a beautiful person, inside and out," said Eugene. "You picked a good one. Then again, if memory serves me, you've loved Elizabeth since high school."

"I'm glad she's back in my life," said Rick. "I am so grateful to be able to love her forever."

"Wow, Ric'O, that's quite a statement," said Eugene.

"How else would you love a wife?" asked Rick.

"I don't know," said Eugene. "I've never had one, and I've never met anyone who promotes that depth of feeling. Admiration? Yes. Attraction? Oh, yes. 'Love for forever?' Mmmm, I don't think so. Ric'O, that goes beyond "til death do us part.'"

"It's how I feel," said Rick.

"Apparently," said Eugene. "Well, congratulations, because that is something I can definitely pass on to the family."

"The family?" asked Rick.

"Yes," said Eugene, "you know how they always want the backstory."

"Backstory."

"Yes, for funerals, they want to know how someone died. For weddings, they want to know if and how that person fell in love – or if they really love at all," said Eugene.

"In that case," said Rick, "go ahead and share it."

"It will make Zietta Nerva happy," said Eugene.

"I'm not sure anything can accomplish that," said Rick, "but please, definitely tell her. Elizabeth is already nervous about meeting her."

"Who wouldn't be?" asked Eugene. "We've been around her our whole lives, but to the uninitiated, Zietta is one challenging handful of determined woman, and the only people who truly matter on this earth are the ones in this family."

Rick let out a small laugh. "I'd laugh harder, but it's basically true."

"Oh, oh, oh, oh!" said Eugene. "I think I caught a fish!"

Chapter Twenty-Five

Elizabeth jumped when her cell phone buzzed.

Hey, Geno and I are back at the restaurant. Want to pop over for a while before I open the place?

She was tempted to tell him to enjoy the rest of his day with his cousin, but she knew that was delaying the inevitable. *Do you need help tonight? I am available and promise not to get angry at anyone who finds you irresistible.*

That would be a nice change, texted Rick. *How was last night?*

Better than I thought it might be, wrote Elizabeth. *It was long, but Mama and baby are doing well. Bridget was such a blessing to have with me!*

Tell me more when you get here. I'm sure Geno would like to hear about it, too.

Elizabeth sighed and texted Bridget. *Heading over to Rick's. Wish me luck.*

Luck was the one-word response.

She took her time walking the five blocks to Rick's Pizza. She loved the cool October breezes, and the colors of Wisconsin's nature that time of year, but she also knew that was only part of the reason for her slower pace. She wanted to see her fiancé and his cousin but was in no hurry to deliver the message she needed to say.

When the bell tinkled upon her entry into the restaurant, Rick and Eugene both looked toward the door.

"Hey, Sweetheart!" said Rick, "for a moment, I thought you

got lost." He pulled her in toward him and gave her a kiss on the cheek. "I've missed you!"

"Good grief," said Eugene. "It's only been a day!"

"I know," said Rick, "way too long."

"You two are something else!" said Eugene. "I think you should get married. That would cure this needing-to-be-together thing."

"Never!" said Rick, and he grabbed Elizabeth closer still. This time, his kiss fell on her mouth.

"My goodness!" said Elizabeth. "We might have to skip a day every so often just so I can get this kind of greeting when I return!"

"Not happening, Bets," said Rick

Elizabeth smiled, but the tilt of that smile held a wisp on sadness.

"You ok?" asked Rick.

"Yes, but I need to talk to you," said Elizabeth.

She turned her attention to Eugene. "Are you ok if I steal him away for a little while?"

"Of course," said Eugene. "I want to spend time with both of you, but I don't want to be a killjoy."

"Thanks," said Elizabeth. "Can we take a walk?"

"Sure," said Rick.

As soon as they were outside the front door of the pizza parlor, Rick said, "What's happened?"

She took his hand and began to walk away from the center of town. There were far less businesses and people once they headed east from Rick's.

"I've been trying to think of the best way to say this since yesterday afternoon," said Elizabeth. "I'm not finding anything. So, here goes."

She took a deep inhale. "The good news is I know who gave us those candlesticks. The bad news is that you aren't going to like the answer."

"Was it someone who couldn't really afford them?" asked Rick.

"No," said Elizabeth, "I'm pretty sure he can afford them."

"Ok, you said 'he,'" said Rick.

"Yes."

"There's only one 'he' that I know I-. Wait. It's not." Rick stopped walking, dropped her hand, and turned to face her. "Please tell me it's not Randy."

Elizabeth pursed her lips shut.

"Bets, you'd better give me the rest of this story because right now, I don't know if I'm moderately upset, extremely mad, or worried about your safety. Is he a kook or what? I thought you made yourself clear to him the last time he popped into town."

"He's not a kook, and you don't need to worry about my safety," said Elizabeth. "The story I got was that he didn't want it to be any sort of pull to get me back with him, only to show that he wished us well."

"Fine," said Rick. "He could have done that via a verbal wish through a third party."

"He did it this way," said Elizabeth. "It's very typical 'Randy.' He often shows his feelings through gifts."

"He can check his feelings at the door, Bets," said Rick. "I don't much care about them. Are you sure he's not nuts?"

Elizabeth chuckled, just a little. "He's one of the most stable people you've ever met. He wouldn't hurt me, Rick, not in the way you're thinking; and he wouldn't hurt you."

Rick bore his eyes into hers. "Do you still love him?"

"Oh, come on, Rick! You know better than that!" said Elizabeth. "I've loved you forever."

"And yet, you were with him for six years," said Rick.

"Don't blame all that on me," said Elizabeth. "You could have reached out to find where the truth was in that incident all those years ago, but you didn't."

"Neither did you."

"Ok, we were both stupid not to talk it out," said Elizabeth. "That's part of why I'm telling you this. I didn't want it to be another 'Vicky' situation. I didn't want a wedge driven between us where there didn't need to be. I wanted you to know right away. No secrets. No surprises."

"That's one wallop of a surprise," said Rick. "How did he even know when our wedding was?"

"Friends from Madison," said Elizabeth.

"Of course," said Rick. "Sometimes I hate that town. They're a little too gabby for my taste."

"Really?" said Elizabeth. "Do you think if Randy lived in Pineville, or had friends here, that he wouldn't have heard when our wedding was happening?"

"Everyone knows everything in this town," said Rick.

"That's my point. No matter in which town we had lived, he would have heard about it," said Elizabeth.

"Ok, all right," said Rick. "If you say you are physically safe from him, I will be cautiously watchful. You know him far better than me, or at least you think you do. I also believe that he didn't have to try too hard to find out when we are getting married."

She took his hand in hers and started to walk again. She was silent.

"You don't think this conversation is over, do you?" asked Rick.

"I was hoping it was," said Elizabeth. "What more do you want to know or say?"

"I'm still deciding how angry I am," said Rick.

"Do you love me?" asked Elizabeth.

"Don't *ever* ask me that again!" said Rick. His voice rocked with anger.

"What's wrong now?" asked Elizabeth.

"Apparently, I'm not the only one who does," said Rick, "and that, I don't like."

"I can't control that any more than you can control those women who come into your restaurant to drool over you more than your lasagna," said Elizabeth.

Rick stopped. He still held Elizabeth's hand, which also forced her to stop. His eyes went into slits.

"Is this why you said what you did about helping out at the restaurant without getting jealous?" asked Rick. "Do you even think the two are comparable?"

"Well," Elizabeth said, a hint of hesitancy crept into her voice. "I think they are."

"Are you crazy?" asked Rick. "How can you even begin to think some strange women that I've never met, don't know from Adam, and may never see again, can compare to your former, long-term, can't take 'no' for an answer boyfriend, or shall we call him your fiancé? Which do you prefer, Elizabeth?"

Tears welled in Elizabeth's eyes. "Don't call me Elizabeth! You know how that hurts me."

"What do you think you're doing to me right now?" asked Rick. "Don't you think there's an element of 'hurt' here? There's not a single, reasonable comparison you can make between these two things. Yet, here you stand, trying to get me to believe that strangers being silly with a night out with their friends is any way the same as an ex-love sending anonymous presents for a wedding. How stupid do you think I am?"

"I don't think you're stupid at all, and you know that," said Elizabeth.

"What you're attempting to do is to make light of this to the point of being ludicrous," said Rick.

"No, I'm not," said Elizabeth. "I guess I don't see it the way you do."

"Probably not," said Rick, "but you also don't see it the way you are trying to get me to see it, either. You're lying to me."

"I am not lying!" said Elizabeth. "I've told you the truth, and I told you all I know about it. Rick, you've got to believe that, please!"

"I believe that part of it," said Rick, "but there's no way you are going to get me to believe the rest. It's simply not the way things are."

"So, what do you want me to say?" asked Elizabeth, "that Randy will love me for the rest of his life, that he wants me back in his life, and that because of that, I want you to focus on how childish and jealous I was when those women were flirting with you?"

Rick let go of her hand. A wind kicked up, and he brushed his hair out of his eyes. "There's the real answer," he said.

"I was just blowing things out of proportion for emphasis!" said Elizabeth.

"No, you weren't," said Rick. "That's the real story whether you want to admit it or not."

"Rick, come on," said Elizabeth. "It's hyperbole!"

Rick shook his head. "It's not. It's exactly how you wanted me to focus. You didn't want me to draw the true comparison, only for me to mentally level the field and pretend they were one and the same."

"I am no longer with Randy," said Elizabeth, "and if you remember, I broke up with him many months before we started dating again. I also told him that you and I were going to get married the last time I saw him. We left it on a good note, nothing more than that."

"You know he still loves you," said Rick.

"I know he *did*," said Elizabeth.

"He still does," said Rick.

"I don't know that," said Elizabeth.

"Yes, you do," said Rick. "That's part of what is annoying me right now. You are still pretending, to me at least, that you have no idea how much you still mean to him. You want me to pretend he's just some nice friend from your past."

"Can't we call him that?" asked Elizabeth. "Why must you make more out of it than it is?"

Rick let out a deep sigh. "You can't get past what you won't acknowledge."

"Meaning what?" asked Elizabeth.

Rick put up his hand in a stopping gesture. "The words going through my mind right now aren't civil. I want to finish this walk and think."

"Ok, let's just walk," said Elizabeth. "We don't have to talk about it anymore."

"Oh, yes, we do," said Rick, "but not right now. I'm at the verge of losing my temper. I don't want to do that."

"Can I walk with you?" asked Elizabeth.

"Not right now," said Rick. "Please, go back to Yarkton House, or wherever it is you were going to go after you left me today. I'll text you in the morning."

"So, we're still ok?" asked Elizabeth.

"I don't know," said Rick, "probably. Let me work this out in my head."

Chapter Twenty-Six

Buses were uncommon in Pineville. The sight of the large silver one brought shoppers and shopkeepers out from the businesses and onto Main Street.

"When did we get on the bus route?" asked one man.

"Maybe it's some sort of celebrity," said a woman who was obviously hoping that was the case.

"Most likely, someone got lost," said a man.

"None of the above," said Rick.

"How do you know that?" asked the woman.

"They're my relatives," said Rick.

"Your relatives?" said the woman. "Why in the world are they on a bus?"

"My family is efficient," said Rick. "They all planned on getting to the airport within a few hours of each other. The ones who arrived early waited. Those who arrived late hustled. One bus, and the family, except for those who are driving in for the wedding, are here."

Rick and Eugene stepped from in front of the restaurant and closer toward the bus to greet their relatives.

"But the wedding isn't until Saturday!" said the woman.

"Yes, but they were not about to pay for two buses. Everybody comes at once, or they rent a car," said Rick. "Our family has traveled to weddings like that for years."

"You mean there's more coming?" asked one of the men.

Rick chuckled. "Yes, about double this amount."

"Oh, good heavens!" said the woman. "Where are they all

staying?"

"Anywhere there's room," said Rick.

Elizabeth was at his side before the first Polisari deboarded the bus.

"Good morning," said Rick. He gave her a short kiss.

"Good morning, Miss Elizabeth," said Eugene.

"Good morning," said Elizabeth. "I see the first wave has arrived."

The driver began unloading luggage from the bottom compartment of the bus. One look inside the space had Elizabeth dialing her cell phone. "Michael?" she said. "Grab whoever is available and come over to Rick's, please. There's enough luggage in the bottom of this bus to fill a 747."

Elizabeth felt as though she was in a pre-wedding receiving line. Each person hugged or kissed her, Rick, and Eugene, as they got off the bus. Her head was spinning with names and how each person was related to her fiancé.

"I'm never going to remember all of this," Elizabeth whispered in Rick's ear.

"You aren't expected to do that," said Rick. "You'll learn all the names over time, just like people do with your family."

"I don't have this many relatives!" said Elizabeth.

"Maybe not," said Rick, "but you have darn near this many in Pineville alone."

"Haha," said Elizabeth.

Eugene elbowed Rick. "Here she comes."

"Here who comes?" asked Elizabeth.

Rick and Eugene both walked as close as possible to the front door of the bus. They each held out a hand to the formidable woman descending the stairs.

"Zietta Nerva!" said Rick. He gave her a kiss on the cheek. "It's so good to see you again!"

"Oh, my Ricardo!" she said. She hugged him tight. "You look good!"

"Hi, Zietta!" said Eugene. "I haven't seen you in over a year! When am I getting some of your delicious calamari?"

"Eugene," she said with a lot less enthusiasm. "You come to my house. I'll make you calamari. You don't come? I don't make it for you."

She pointed to two large suitcases. "You boys get my luggage."

"Yes, Zietta," said both Rick and Eugene.

They walked toward her bags, weaving around other suitcases that were being pulled out from the under compartment.

"I see she hasn't changed," said Rick.

"Did you think she would?" asked Eugene.

A few cars pulled up to the curb behind the bus.

"We're here!" said Michael.

"Good grief," said Deke. "How much luggage do these folks need for a weekend?"

Michael eyed the sidewalk where the bus driver was now closing the compartment. "About that much, I guess."

Joseph pulled up in his squad car. He walked over to Rick and Elizabeth who were trying to usher all the family inside the restaurant.

"Dad's inside!" said Rick. "Grab a seat, everyone, and we'll figure out where and when everyone is going. In the meantime, there's food, soda, and beer coming out!"

"What are you doing here, Joseph?" asked Elizabeth.

"Well, I heard about it, but I had to come see it for myself," Joseph said.

"You mean the bus?" asked Rick. "I thought I told you about that."

"You did," said Joseph, "but I also heard about the luggage. I've seen less on overseas flights."

"That's my family," said Rick. "Traveling light isn't in the wedding repertoire."

"I can see that," said Joseph. "You want some help getting this off the street?"

"I don't think that's exactly in your job description," said Rick.

"Did someone complain?" asked Elizabeth.

"No," said Joseph, "but it is causing quite a few looks in this direction."

"Are you Elizabeth's brother?" asked Eugene.

"Yes, I'm Joseph," he said.

Eugene extended his hand. "I'm Rick's cousin."

"Eugene?" Joseph asked.

"Yes, how did you know that?" asked Eugene.

"Wild guess," said Joseph. "Actually, I saw you walking with Rick yesterday. I knew you were the one arriving early."

Joseph excused himself and walked back to his squad car. He called in his location.

"Whatever reason did you give them for being here?" asked Eugene.

Joseph nodded at all the suitcases on the sidewalk. "Helping to clear a traffic jam on Main Street."

It was a couple of hours and lots of pizzas, calzones, and ravioli later before everyone was escorted to their various hotels, relatives' houses, friends' houses, the campground cabins, and the Yarkton House. Everyone in Elizabeth's immediate family, and several other friends and relatives, helped the guests get settled.

Eugene came back toward the end of the restaurant's hours to help Rick clean.

"Geno, you're a guest, too," said Rick. "You do not need to do this."

"Look," said Eugene, "I have spent the afternoon and most of tonight with the rest of the family. Frankly, they've all traveled today, and they're tired. Secondly, I want to think I'm your favorite cousin. We're the only two in this family who didn't have siblings. That makes us rare. We need to bond over that."

Rick laughed. "You're a little crazy, you know that?" He handed him a bottle of cleaner and a rag. "Beyond that, you're pretty amazing. I think I really needed you to be here this week.

Thank you."

"Oh, now you stop that," said Eugene. "It'll go to my head."

When the bell over the front door tinkled, Rick looked up from cleaning the kitchen counter. It was almost precisely the time when he usually locked the door. He didn't expect to see anyone, much less Elizabeth, come in the restaurant.

"Hey, what are you doing here?" he asked. "Everything all right?"

"That's what I came to ask you," she said. Elizabeth came over to him and grabbed another cleaning cloth to help.

"Ric'O, how about if I clean the dining area, and leave this greasy mess to you two?" said Eugene.

Rick nodded.

"Thank you, Eugene," said Elizabeth.

Eugene said nothing more but headed off to the cleaning closet to get what was needed for the Rick's Pizza dining area.

"I appreciate the cleaning help," said Rick, "but I don't have a solid answer for you."

"How mad are you?" Elizabeth asked.

He took off his rubber gloves and faced her. "I'm angry. I want to throttle your former whatever-the-heck-you-want-to-call-him. I don't know what is happening between us and why this is so painful and difficult."

"I don't know what else to say to you," said Elizabeth.

He put his gloves back on and went back to his cleaning and disinfecting. "That's where I am, too. Please go home and go to bed. We'll figure out what we need to do, but I can't do that right now."

Elizabeth barely got out a 'good night' to Eugene as she hurried out the front door and down Main Street toward Yarkton House.

Her nerves were shot. Her eyes were burning from holding back tears. Her mind was racing, and she had no idea if she was going to be Elizabeth Polisari in a couple more days, or if she was to remain Elizabeth Anderson.

Chapter Twenty-Seven

Elizabeth didn't know whether to run home or to spend as much time away as possible. She wanted to race up the stairs into her own room and settle in for a good cry followed by some needed rest. Yet, she hoped that none of Rick's family were still downstairs at Yarkton House. The thought of facing any of them made her stomach churn all the more. Dealing with her emotions concerning Rick's anger over the Randy situation was bad enough without worrying about how she appeared to family members that didn't really know her.

She saw the parlor aglow with lights. This time of night, there was usually one light left on in the parlor in the center of the main front window in case any guests wanted to come downstairs. She thought about letting herself in through the back entrance. However. she knew that wouldn't help. There were no steps to the upstairs except the ones that were right inside the front entry hall.

Elizabeth steeled herself. She prayed it was Bridget who was in the parlor. However, Bridget would not have put on all the lights. It was likely she would have only lit a fire in the hearth not light the room one step short of a bus terminal. It had to be the Polisaris.

She had a brief thought of texting Rick to see if he and Eugene would come over and run interference between her and the family. While they might come, Elizabeth knew the emotional state Rick was in and that he wouldn't welcome a text to come rescue her from being the hostess at her own establishment.

Eugene had played host and tour guide all afternoon and was ready to wind down for the night. This was up to her.

She wiped her eyes, plastered what would have to pass for a smile on her face and went inside. The sight of a large group of Rick's family members sitting in her parlor and dining room was more than a surprise; it was somewhat of a shock.

"Oh, my goodness!" said Elizabeth as she looked from one relative to another. "I am so sorry! I didn't know you wanted to get together here this evening."

"I hope you're not upset with us," said one woman. "Your assistant said you would be happy to have us here."

"No, yes," said Elizabeth, "I mean, of course, you're welcome to be here! I'm only upset that I wasn't here to greet all of you."

"You greet us now," said Zietta Nerva.

Elizabeth nodded. "Yes, I will. Give me just one moment, please. I'll be right back."

She went into the downstairs bathroom and splashed some cold water on her face. "Like it or not, buddy," she said under her breath. "I'm texting you. You can go back to hating me tomorrow. Tonight, you are a Polisari and the host of this weekend."

You have about two dozen relatives in my parlor. If you are still awake, and I pray you are, can you and Eugene come over here, please? I think they would really rather spend time with you than me.

She tapped her fingers rhythmically on the counter for what seemed like forever. "Come on, come on," she whispered.

Her phone pinged. *On our way. Dad is coming, too.*

She made her way back to the crowd. She began with those seated in her dining room. She stopped at each person to welcome them to both her home and the wedding weekend.

She worked her way into the parlor itself. She was getting closer and closer to Zietta Nerva. She knew better than to avoid talking to Rick's aunt. That would be tantamount to disrespect. Neither Elizabeth nor the Polisari family would be pleased with such an offense.

Please, please, please get here, she thought to herself as she made her way from person-to-person, getting nearer and nearer to the family's matriarch.

Rick still had not arrived when she approached the one person she was nervous about meeting.

"Zietta Nerva," said Elizabeth, "did you have a good afternoon and evening?"

"I was with family," said Zietta Nerva. "You did not come by."

Give me the right words, God, she thought. "I thought perhaps you would enjoy catching up with the relatives. I know how they all want to be with you."

One of Nerva's daughters, who was standing behind her mother, gave Elizabeth a sly smile. She didn't say a word, but her look conveyed the sentiment. *I know what you're doing.*

"Chiara," Zietta said to the woman, "you get Elizabeth a chair. We need to have a chat."

Elizabeth's stomach rumbled out loud. She prayed nobody else heard it.

One of the men in the room arose from his chair and brought it over to Elizabeth. "Here you go," he said. "I'm going to be heading out soon. It's been a long day."

He leaned over and kissed Nerva on the cheek. "Buon anotte, Zietta."

Nerva touched his hand. "You be here on time to drive us to the diner. We have a reservation for the family."

"Yes, I will be here."

Rick, Eugene, and Rick, Sr. came in the front door.

"Hey, you don't invite me?" said Rick, Sr. "You come to my town. Come to my beautiful Betsy's inn, but you don't invite me?"

"Ricardo," said Zietta Nerva, "we did not know if you were helping Ricky tonight. We know business is business. We would see you tomorrow morning. Yes?"

"Of course, you will," said Rick, Sr. "Ricky's grown up now. He doesn't need me too often. We sit and talk."

Rick's dad turned his attention toward Elizabeth. "How

about you let an old man sit there?" Since his back was to Nerva for the moment, he winked at Elizabeth.

"Certainly," said Elizabeth. "I still have some other people to say hello to. If you'll excuse me, Zietta."

"Hm," said Zietta, but she waved her away.

Nerva looked at Rick's dad. "That girl looks like a big balloon of nerves; one more thing, and she will pop. She did not even run to Ricky when he came in the door. Are You sure she loves him the way she should? You know the romance cools over time. They must be very much in love to make things work beyond the honeymoon. Otherwise, all arguments and tension, no love."

Elizabeth heard part of Nerva's comments, but she was grateful to be away from the one Polisari who was most likely to not care for her.

She saw Eugene next. She hugged him. "Thank you so much for coming," she whispered in his ear. "I was overwhelmed with Polisaris."

"And with Zietta Nerva's scrutiny?" he asked.

"I don't think she likes me," said Elizabeth.

"Your tension is radiating off of you like a force field, Elizabeth," said Eugene. "She picks up on that. Heck, I picked up on that, and I can be clueless."

She backed up and looked him straight in the eye. "Oh, Eugene, I think you are anything but clueless. I think you know exactly what's going on with each person. I would call you insightful to the point of being shrewd."

"Shrewd?" said Eugene. "That could be taken as an insult."

"You know it's not," said Elizabeth. "Zietta Nerva may be intuitive in how she sees people for how they appear, but I think you are intuitive in how you see people for who they really are."

"Why, Miss Elizabeth," said Eugene in a feigned Southern accent, "I do believe you give me honor in your words."

Elizabeth gave him a smile. "Yes, I am so glad you came to Pineville early. I think you have been the greatest gift for which Rick could have hoped."

Eugene let out a short chuckle. "Interesting."

"What is?" asked Elizabeth.
"Rick said the same thing to me earlier."

Chapter Twenty-Eight

If it was a scenic spot in Pineville, Eugene took their pictures. He had sunrise shots at the banks of, and on a beautiful little bridge over, the Huhawira River with only the bride and groom. Eugene's eye for calibrating the perfect shot was incredible. He choreographed sleepy poses, silly poses, happy poses, and loving ones.

Elizabeth could tell by the way Rick responded to the suggestions that he was in complete agreement with the compositions. That alone brought comfort to Elizabeth. Rick was an avid and accomplished photographer in his own right. Knowing that he never once contradicted or questioned his cousin's directions told Elizabeth that Eugene was at least as good as Rick with a camera, if not better.

After having breakfast with the entire group at her parents' diner, the bridal party joined them for the rest of the picture-taking day.

"The first stop will be where we already are," said Eugene as they all gathered in the Pineville Diner and Campground parking lot. "We are heading into the campground! Elizabeth, lead the way to every pretty little spot you know here."

There were shots in the trees. The oaks, elms, maples, and pines provided different color palettes and showed the beauty of the land.

"I have a lot of ideas for this area," said Eugene as he pondered the scenery around him. "However, I do have a question for you, Elizabeth."

"What's that?" asked Elizabeth.

"Is there a way we could get a pile of these leaves for the little ones?" asked Eugene. "I would love to have a few shots of the kids playing in them. Those colors command, and they can be shown for their majesty, as well as their fun."

"I don't like being called 'little' anymore," said Charlie.

"Charlton!" said his father, Joseph. "That was rude."

"Sorry," said Charlie.

"Do you still like playing in leaves," said Eugene, "or are you getting too big for that, too?"

"I love jumping in leaves!" said Charlie.

"It's one of the best parts of fall!" said Emmie.

"Then, we're good," said Eugene. "How about it, Miss Elizabeth? Do you think we can get a good-sized stack of these put together?"

"I think so," said Elizabeth.

"I'll go get some rakes and a blower from the shed," said Michael. "It will take a me a few minutes, though."

"No worries," said Eugene, "I'll do the bride and groom shots while you're gone."

As soon as Michael returned with the rakes and blower, Joseph, Lucas, and Michael set to work on building the pile for the children. It was an effort to keep the kids from running through the blowing and gathering leaves until the pile was the best size for being captured in photography. Once the kids' leaf shots were done, they were allowed to continue to play in them until they were needed for some other group shots.

Eugene took multiple shots of people peeking from behind campground trees. There were shots of a few brave folks climbing them or hanging out of them. He caught a few candid moments of people talking to one another, laughing, or even pondering something. Rick's cousin knew his way around a camera, but he also knew how to pose people, catch them at their finest, and find ways to keep rambunctious kids entertained.

The group moved on to other locations around town finishing at Roosevelt Park. It was about mid-afternoon, and the children left to go home, while many of the adults in the wedding party went on to find a place to play cards, backgammon, or simply relax. The ones who remained were the ones who began, Rick, Elizabeth, and Eugene.

"Ok, guys," said Eugene, "Other than some sunset shots to wrap up the day, are there any other places you want to photograph? Any super gorgeous spots we missed, or anything that has a special significance for the two of you?"

"Just one," said Rick. "Follow me."

He led the three of them back through the winding paths and grassy areas of the park. Elizabeth knew where Rick was headed. She was hoping she was wrong.

She saw the bench come into view. That bench. Their bench. She stopped. "No. This is cruel, Rick."

"What's the matter with you, Bets?" Rick asked.

"How can you bring me here when you are still thinking about calling off the wedding?" she asked.

Eugene left most of his gear on the ground and walked a short distance away from the two of them, ostensibly to get some shots of the trees in the park.

Rick took her by the arm. "What's wrong with you? Why do you think I'm the one who wants to stay single? I've told you from the beginning of this second phase of our relationship how much I love you."

"Yes, but you said you had to think about the Randy thing," said Elizabeth.

"Sure, I do," said Rick. "That doesn't mean I want to call off the wedding."

"You don't?" asked Elizabeth.

"Sometimes I swear you are out of your ever-loving mind!" said Rick.

"You've been giving me mixed signals all week!" said Elizabeth.

"I don't think so," said Rick.

"Well, then you'd better revisit your thinking," said Elizabeth. "You told me you were angry."

"Of course, I am," said Rick. "The guy is a clueless moron."

"That's not how I would describe him," said Elizabeth.

"Well, how would you?!" said Rick. His voice was getting louder.

Eugene came back over. "Look," he said, "I'm all for people working out their own problems, but the sun is going to set soon, and I want to get these last shots in. If you're going to break up, do it after I'm done, ok?"

Rick and Elizabeth snapped out of their argument and headed over toward the bench. Rick picked up one of the legs of it to check to see if their carved initials were still there. "Yep, this is it."

"Good," said Eugene, "now, do that one more time, and I'll capture the shot."

Rick obliged.

"Now, Elizabeth, you get your pretty face over here," said Eugene. "We need to capture that love that Zietta Nerva wants to see."

She stood next to Rick, arms at her sides.

"What exactly is that supposed to be?" asked Eugene. "I could get more romantic pictures from two strangers."

"Sorry," said Elizabeth.

"Yeah," said Rick.

Eugene put his camera down and walked closer. "Sit," he said.

"Which one of us?" asked Rick.

"Both of you. Sit!" said Eugene.

Elizabeth looked at Rick, who looked at Eugene.

"What?" asked Rick.

"Now," said Eugene, "I am not going to have you two ruining my reputation as a photographer or as a family member."

"What's that got to do with anything?" asked Rick.

"You two are about as unromantic as they come right now. The pictures will show that. You can't hide anger or mistrust," said Eugene.

"Wait a minute," said Rick. "Who said I don't trust her?"

"What about you, Princess Elizabeth?" asked Eugene. "Do

you trust my cousin, Ric'O?"

"Of course, I do," said Elizabeth.

"Well, baby doll, it's not showing," said Eugene. "You look like you're afraid he's going to bolt and run."

"I would never do that to her!" said Rick.

"But, you're hop-skipping angry at some thing or another," said Eugene.

"Those stupid candlesticks," said Rick. "It's nothing more than being angry that her ex-boyfriend can't seem to get Elizabeth out of his mind."

"So, you're jealous," said Eugene.

"No, he's clueless," said Rick.

"What's the deal about the candlesticks, Elizabeth?" asked Eugene. "Ric'O tends to leave out a few details."

"Oh," she sighed, "my former boyfriend sent them to us as a wedding gift."

"Ok," said Eugene. "Why did that make you so angry?"

"Are you serious?" asked Rick. "That's my future wife, and this guy, this guy who was anything but thoughtful of her feelings when they were dating, sends her an expensive present."

"Do you resent that he spent money?" asked Eugene.

"I don't care about his money, one way or the other," said Rick. "After all, that's all he was good at back when they were together. Climb that corporate ladder."

"So, you're just the pizza man, and he's the executive," said Eugene.

"Eugene!" said Elizabeth. "That's horribly unkind! I don't see Rick that way at all! He knows that."

"The question is, does he see himself that way?" said Eugene. "Elizabeth, you have far less to do with this than you think. You told him the truth, and you told him very soon after you knew. If I know my cousin, he would find that honorable."

"Of course, I do," said Rick.

"Then what gives?" said Eugene. "Why the raw anger? You were spewing love the other night. How you wanted to love this woman, 'forever.' Not just until you died, but forever. Did you mean that, or was that a cute catchphrase to haul out for my benefit?"

"I don't do anything for your benefit, Eugene," said Rick.

"Ah," said Eugene, "now I'm *Eugene*. That means you are ticked at me, too."

"I'm ticked at a lot of people right now," said Rick.

"Get over your finest self," said Eugene. "You run a restaurant. It's a pizza place – and then some. Embrace that. You aren't likely to climb a corporate ladder unless you start a chain. That's not likely since you would be hard-pressed to find a group of people who could fill all the roles you perform on a daily basis."

"A franchise situation isn't happening, and we both know it," said Rick. "This is definitely a family restaurant in a small town."

"Are you jealous that Randy's career is going to take him further? That he likely earns more money than you?" asked Eugene. "Are you jealous that he would be able to give Elizabeth more than you can?"

"Eugene, please," said Elizabeth, who was now in tears. "Stop it! I don't care about those kinds of things. I want Rick. I want this town. I want the life we will build together."

Rick put his arm around Elizabeth and pulled her in close to his chest. "Stop," he said to his cousin. "You've made your point."

"Can I take these pictures now?" asked Eugene. "We've got about thirty minutes of good light."

He snapped picture after picture, capturing more emotions than even he knew would emerge on camera.

After they finished the day and had headed back to Rick's, Eugene excused himself to go up to Rick, Sr.'s upstairs apartment. He stopped a couple steps up the staircase. "Ric'O, one question."

"Yes."

"Was I wrong about how you felt?" asked Eugene.

"No," said Rick, "and I both thank you and hate you for bringing all that up."

Chapter Twenty-Nine

The old, clapboard Pineville Community Church had hosted a multitude of weddings over its hundred-plus year history. Pastor Wilbur Plain had presided at well over one hundred to date in his tenure there. Similar, sometimes identical, words were spoken. There was a wedding party and most often music to accompany what the couple wished to convey to those who came to witness their union.

Yet, each wedding was unique. That day's marital ceremony for Elizabeth Anderson and Ricardo Polisari, Jr. would have its own stamps of remembrance as well. The bride, the groom, the wedding party members, as well as each guest would take away whatever touched their heart.

In the bride's room, Elizabeth's sister and maid-of-honor, Angela, was going over details of the day with her, while Bridget fussed over her make-up. Elizabeth's mom, Jeannie, stood off to the side, marveling at how beautiful her eldest daughter looked on her wedding day. Stephanie fussed over her four young children, attempting to keep them clean and dry. Julia cooed at her young daughter and played peak-a-boo to keep her laughing. Melissa, the bridesmaid from the Polisari side, stood in the background, smiling at the wonderful, busy sight. Eugene caught all the high points and emotions on camera.

In the groom's room, Rick, Lucas, and Michael were sitting at a table talking. Eugene came in and caught a few quick shots, but it was apparent that the action was on the female side of the group.

"I hope Joseph gets back on time," said Lucas. "I don't want to see Angela walk down that aisle alone."

"If it comes to that," said Rick, "I'll draft one of my other cousins. She doesn't need to be by herself."

"That's law enforcement," said Michael. "I guess there really aren't any holidays or times you can count on to get time completely for yourself."

"Did he say exactly what the problem was?" asked Rick.

"No," said Lucas. "He just told me to let you know he would be back on time. However, he did need to handle something."

"Ok, we're getting pretty tight on time," said Rick.

"If Joseph said he would be back," said Michael, "if at all possible, he will be. One thing I will say about my oldest brother, he's a man of his word."

Chapter Thirty

He had parked on a small road near where the highway met Main Street.

"I've got to tell you," said Joseph, "you are one of the last people on Earth I thought I would be talking to today."

"You're not happy I'm here," said the man. "I know that."

"No," said Joseph, "I'm not. Now, what can I do for you? I have a sister who's getting married today, and I won't be late for her service."

"I want to talk to you about that," said the man opposite him, "and I want to talk about the future."

"Look, let me give you the facts so there will be no room for misinterpretation. Fact one, my sister is getting married in less than an hour to a man she's loved for a long time. Fact two, you're not him. Fact three, you caused a real hornet's nest a week or so ago. Fact four, Elizabeth's future is with Rick Polisari and most likely in Pineville, Wisconsin. Not Atlanta. Not Denver. Not LA. Pineville – with her family. Fact five, you are not invited to today's events or any others. Have I made myself clear?"

"Yes," said the man. "Can I say what I came to say now?"

"You were just here in March. Why didn't you say it then?" said Joseph.

"Things have changed," the man said.

"Do tell," said Joseph.

"Let me address your facts. Then, I will add a few of my own, if you don't mind," said the man.

"As long as you make it quick," said Joseph. "I intend to be out of here in ten minutes or less. You will drive away before I do."

The man nodded. "Fact one, as you put it, I know Elizabeth is getting married today. I have no intention of disrupting that."

"That's a good start," said Joseph.

"Fact two, I am fully aware that she's marrying that Rick guy. How long she's loved him, and whether that took a hiatus when we were together, I don't know, and I'm not sure I want to know."

"I'm not going there," said Joseph, "and I would suggest you stop torturing yourself with questions like those."

"Your fact three was about the present," said the man. "It is simply a gift. There are no strings attached to it, and I'm guessing Elizabeth already figured that out. She knows me better than anyone."

"Get off that track," said Joseph. "You're not helping yourself, and you're starting to irritate me."

"Fact four, I've known for a long time that Elizabeth's heart was in Pineville."

"Yes, it is," said Joseph.

"Fact five, I am not stupid enough to believe that my invitation was lost in the mail. I know my presence is not wanted."

"Then, why are you here, Randy," said Joseph, "and of all the people in this family, why did you want to talk to me? Our history has never been pleasant. Frankly, you'd be hard-pressed to find anyone in this family who loathes you as much as I do."

"I'm here because I had to show myself what my stupidity cost me," said Randy.

"You could have figured that out in Indiana or wherever it is that you're living now," said Joseph.

"No," said Randy, "I needed to fully know this. I needed to show myself that I lost the one person in my life who would have been there for me through thick and thin."

"Too bad you didn't feel the same way," said Joseph. "You were never here when she wanted you to be. You were so busy consuming yourself with work that you didn't concern yourself with her."

"Or with our relationship," added Randy. "Look, Joseph, I know all that. I was a workaholic fool who thought as long as I kept progressing, Elizabeth would keep loving me."

"For Elizabeth, one has nothing to do with the other," said Joseph.

"I know that now," said Randy.

"You didn't come here to try to convince me to stop this wedding, did you?" asked Joseph.

"No, but I made a promise to Elizabeth, and through all of this, I have determined that I won't be able to keep it," said Randy.

"What's that?" asked Joseph.

"I promised her that I would always let her know where I was so that if she ever did need me in the future, for anything at all, she could always get in touch with me," said Randy.

"She can live with you not fulfilling that promise," said Joseph.

"The thing is, I can't," said Randy.

"I thought you just said you knew you couldn't do it," said Joseph.

"That's where you come in," said Randy.

Joseph blew out a long, loud breath. "I'm confused, and you'd better step this up because I need to leave."

"I want to send those messages to you," said Randy.

"Are you out of your ever-loving mind?" asked Joseph. "Why would I do that for you, and why would you want me to be a part of this?"

"Because despite your hate for me," said Randy, "I know you are a man of honor and honesty. You wouldn't tell me you will do something and then not follow-through."

"And I'm telling you I want no part of it," said Joseph.

"You told me to stop torturing myself," said Randy. "That's what I'm trying to do. I want to write to Elizabeth, email her, call her, and text her. Yet, I know I can't do any of the above without either hurting her or her relationship with her husb-." The word stuck in his throat. "Rick."

"That's admirable, and that's real," said Joseph. "So, don't."

"However," said Randy, "as much as you think I am a first-class heel, I am a man of my promises, too."

"Don't do it," said Joseph.

"Then agree to be my liaison," said Randy. "I will only email you when I relocate. I won't bother you with anything else. I won't ask you how she's doing or to provide me with any details on her life or her family. I simply want to keep my promise to her in a way that won't tear me up inside."

"I'm not comfortable with you contacting her," said Joseph.

"Then be my go-between," said Randy.

"You shouldn't have said that in the first place," said Joseph.

Randy shook his head no. "Maybe not from your perspective, but it is what I needed to do from mine. I also want your sister to know that our relationship did mean more to me than she may realize. She was one of the reasons I wanted so badly to succeed."

"Randy," said Joseph, "it's who you are. You will always go for the next best thing."

"Not with women," said Randy. "I do that with work, yes. With material things, yes. However, I never, ever cheated on your sister when we were dating, and I do not, even if I am not the best at them, take relationships lightly."

"All right," said Joseph. "I really do have to go now." He scribbled an email address on a sheet of paper from a small notebook he always carried with him. "You can send new addresses there. Also, do not call the department in the future. That is for actual departmental work, not meeting up with my sister's old boyfriend."

"Understood," said Randy.

"Goodbye, Randy," said Joseph.

"Take care of her, Joseph," said Randy.

"Rick will do that," said Joseph.

Randy's voice was hoarse. "But if something ever comes up that she needs someone to help her-"

"You're doing it to yourself again, Randy," said Joseph. "Those kinds of statements are going to haunt you on your way home. Leave with a good thought, not one that's going to chew you up."

"I am," said Randy. He swallowed, and his voice returned to normal. "I'm leaving here knowing that she has everything she ever really wanted, her family, her town, and Rick. All I really want for Elizabeth is for her to have what she loves. As hard as this is for me, I know she does."

Randy got into his car. He rolled down the window. "Oh, and one thing I really am looking forward to."

Joseph continued to lean against his car. "What's that?"

"I will never have to count, or smell, the cows on that highway again," said Randy.

He took one last look at the sheriff. "Thanks, Joseph – and goodbye."

Joseph waited until he saw Randy's car turn onto the highway before he went back to the church.

Chapter Thirty-One

Joseph hurried over to the groom's room. "I'm here," he said.

"You barely made it on time," said Rick, "but I'm sure glad you did."

"Are you done working now, Daddy?" asked Charlie.

"I think so," said Joseph.

"Everything ok?" asked Rick.

Joseph avoided the question. "How did Charlie get over here?"

"Mom brought me," said Charlie. "She said I need to walk with the men."

"Yes, you do," said Joseph.

There was a knock on the groom's room door.

"Yes?" said Rick.

"You should line up now," said the minister.

"Thank you," said Rick.

"Joseph, Lucas, Michael, Charlie," said Rick.

"Where do you go?" asked Charlie.

"I'm in the back because the brides are always the last ones to come down the aisle," said Rick.

"But, you're not a bride," said Charlie.

The guys let out some tension-relieving laughter.

"No, but I'm going to be with the bride," said Rick.

"Let's go," said Joseph. "Dad started playing the entry music."

As the best man, Joseph led the way from the side chamber into the right front of the sanctuary. He did a quick scan of who was in the pews. He believed that Randy had left Pineville, but he also wanted to be sure he hadn't been conned into believing that he was only wanting Elizabeth to be happy.

Rick's cousin, Melissa, smiled all the way down the aisle. It was apparent she was happy to be a part of the day's festivities. Rick smiled at his cousin. She was such a good person and deserved to be respected and cared about for being herself, not just Trisha's sister.

Michael was Melissa's counterpart in the bridal party. He made a dramatic show of extending his arm to her when he met her in the aisle. He smiled broadly. "You look lovely," he said.

Melissa's smile became even wider. "Thank you."

The next bridesmaid to take her walk to the church front was Bridget. The soft yellow of the dress fabric set off her carrot-red hair. The baby's breath that Elizabeth had asked to be woven somehow into their hair was incredible on her. Her natural curls and the delicate flowers were a perfect match for her.

Lucas went forward to escort Bridget to her spot in front of the pulpit. He was honored to be a part of his sister's wedding, especially since she was marrying one of his best friends. He was equally honored that his baby daughter would be toddling down the aisle with his wife. When he went back to the groom's row, he craned his neck to see if he could see either of them.

Angela was next. She looked beautiful in the soft yellow dress Elizabeth had chosen for her bridesmaids. Angela always took her duties seriously. She had looked through bridal magazines and online groups to find out exactly what a maid of honor should do. She had fluffed out Elizabeth's train right before she had grabbed her bouquet and came down the center aisle of the church she knew.

Joseph met her at the designated spot toward the front of the pews and walked her to the left side in front of the elevated pulpit. He then went to his spot in the grooms' row. He did another scan. *So far, so good,* he thought.

Next came Emmie, who was met by her brother, Charlie.

Then came all three of the Anderson babies. Margaret walked and held her mother, Julia's, hand, while Joseph and Stephanie's twins were rolled down the aisle in their stroller, which was decorated in soft versions of the autumn colors. Stephanie beamed with pride from behind the stroller, while Joseph watched them from the front.

The music switched to the official bridal march.

The guests stood as Elizabeth made her entrance in an elegant gown of ivory satin, beaded with pearls. The veil also had some pearls interspersed in the netting. She was a vision of beauty.

Rick swallowed the lump in his throat and went forward to meet his bride. "I love you, Bets," he said softly.

"I love you, too," said Elizabeth.

He took her hand and led her to the center front where Pastor Plain was now standing.

"Dearly beloved," the minister began, "we are gathered here today to witness the uniting of Ricardo Salvatore Polisari, Jr. and Elizabeth Jeannie Anderson. The couple has chosen several Bible verses they wish to share with you. Each has special meaning to them. Some were chosen by the groom, most by the bride-."

Light laughter carried throughout the sanctuary.

"And a few by the presenters themselves," said the minister. "Let us begin by hearing from our best man, Elizabeth's oldest brother, Joseph."

Joseph stepped to the microphone. He looked across the congregation, noting faces along the way. "Pastor almost always uses this passage in his wedding services. It's obvious as to why. I asked his permission to be the one to read it today." He nodded toward the minister. "Thank you, Pastor."

He looked at his note card. "My message for Rick and Elizabeth is quite short but says exactly what I wish to convey to them. Mark 10:9 says:

> "'Therefore what God has joined together, let
> not man separate.'"

Rick squeezed Elizabeth's hand, and Joseph scanned the

sanctuary again as he walked to the groom's row.

The rest of the congregation, unaware of the even deeper meanings for the couple and the sheriff, sung a stanza from a familiar hymn.

Stephanie stepped forward. Being short, she had to stand on a small footstool to see the written cards on the podium, as well as to see the congregation. "For those of you who don't know me, I am Joseph's wife, and the mother of all but one of those beautiful children you saw coming down the aisle."

She smiled. "My reading for today is found in the book of Ecclesiastes, the fourth chapter, verses 9 through 12:

> "'Two *are* better than one,
> "'Because they have a good reward for their
> labor.
> "'For if they fall, one will lift up his companion.
> "'But woe to him *who* is alone when he falls,
> "'For *he has* no one to help him up.
> "'Again, if two lie down together, they will keep
> warm;
> "'But how can one be warm *alone*?
> "'Though one may be overpowered by another,
> two can withstand him.
> "'And a threefold cord is not quickly broken.'"

Zietta Nerva nodded in affirmation of the verse, and the second stanza of the same hymn played as Lucas came forward.

"Hello, everyone, I am Elizabeth's second brother, Lucas. The 'other child' to which Stephanie referred is my beautiful daughter, Margaret. The lovely woman holding her hand is my wife, Julia. I want to welcome you to my sister's wedding and a day for which my family has been waiting for arrival.

"The reading I chose is from the book of Romans, the twelfth chapter, verses 9-13:

> "'Let love *be* without hypocrisy. Abhor what is
> evil. Cling to what is good. *Be* kindly affectionate

to one another in brotherly love, in honor giving preference to one another; not lagging in diligence, fervent in spirit, serving the Lord; rejoicing in hope, patient in tribulation, continuing steadfastly in prayer; distributing to the needs of the saints, given to hospitality.'"

"That sounds very much like the way Julia and Lucas want their marriage to be," Bonnie whispered to Jeannie.

Jeannie nodded.

Don continued to put short verses of loved hymns in between each of the readings. As the church organist, he had played for many weddings. Yet, this was his daughter's wedding, not another townsperson or a stranger – his daughter's. He hung on every word and beamed down from the balcony. His attention was on the podium as the next member of his family came to it.

"I am Julia, Lucas's wife, Margaret's mother, and the other sister-in-law to Elizabeth. When Rick and Elizabeth asked me to read this section of Colossians, I was honored, and I was amazed. I was honored because being included in Elizabeth and Rick's wedding is so special to me. I am also amazed because it says everything I would want to say to the both of them, but so much better, of course."

She slid on her reading glasses and read. "Colossians 3: verses 12-15:

> "'Therefore, as *the* elect of God, holy and beloved, put on tender mercies, kindness, humility, meekness, longsuffering; bearing with one another, and forgiving one another, if anyone has a complaint against another; even as Christ forgave you, so you also *must* do. But above all these things put on love, which is the bond of perfection. And let the peace of God rule in your hearts, to which also you were called in one body; and be thankful.'"

"There we go again," said Bonnie. "Could you describe Julia any better than that?"

Jeannie gave her a sister a look to let her know they could discuss these things later.

Michael was next to the podium. "Hello, I'm Michael, Elizabeth's younger brother, and my mom's favorite child."

Jeannie rolled her eyes at him from the second pew, and then lowered her head.

As many of the people laughed at his often-used joke, Michael said, "In all sincerity, though, I am beyond happy to celebrate this wedding of my sister to Rick. She has loved him for so long, and he has loved her. I have a short reading from 1 Peter 4: verse 8:

"'And above all things have fervent love for one another, for *love will cover a multitude* of sins.'"

Angela handed her bouquet to Bridget as she walked to the altar and stepped up to the microphone. "I am the other sister in the family and the youngest of the five children of my dad and mom. My name is Angela, and there is no one in the world I love more than my big sister, Elizabeth."

Her note cards were already waiting for her. "I want to share a reading from 1 John, chapter 4, verses 16 through the beginning of 17:

"'And we have known and believed the love that God has for us. God is love, and he who abides in love abides in God, and God in him. Love has been perfected among us in this:'"

The two women switched the bridesmaids' bouquets from Bridget's hands to Angela's as Bridget came forward. "Hello, I am Bridget. I work for Elizabeth, and she is also my best friend. I am the only non-family member in this wedding party, and I am incredibly honored to share this day with all of you.

"I am reading from the book of Job. The passage is in chapter 5; verses 24 and 25:

"'You shall know that your tent *is* in peace:

"'You shall visit your dwelling and find nothing amiss.

"'You shall know that descendants *shall* be many,

"'And your offspring like the grass of the earth.'"

When Melissa stepped up to the mic, she said, "I am Rick's cousin, Melissa, and I was thrilled to be asked to be a part of this special day. Thank you, Rick and Elizabeth, for this great privilege. I know you will always be in love.

"Rick has always been wonderful to me. I remember so many conversations he and I have had together, many of them focused on Elizabeth."

She smiled at the couple.

"My reading for today is from Psalms 37: verses 4 and 5:

"'Delight yourself also in the LORD, and He shall give you the desires of your heart.

"'Commit your way to the LORD,

"'Trust also in Him,

"'And He shall bring it to pass.'"

The final bridal party and family reading was done by Eugene. "I am another one of Rick's cousins. My name is Eugene, and when I had the privilege of meeting this beautiful bride earlier in the week, I fell in love. She is the perfect match for my cousin who does not always know where wealth and beauty lie. I have asked Elizabeth's permission to read two complementary passages as she had something else chosen for me to read. She has graciously agreed."

He cleared his throat. "The first reading is from Proverbs 31: 10 through 12:

"'Who can find a virtuous wife?

"'For her worth *is* far above rubies.

"'The heart of her husband safely trusts her;

"'So he will have no lack of gain.

"'She does him good and not evil All the days of
her life.'"

He took a breath and began again. "The second set of verses I want to share is also from Proverbs. This passage is found in chapter 3, verses 15 through 17:

"'She *is* more precious than rubies,
"'And all the things you may desire cannot compare with her.
"'Length of days *is* in her right hand,
"'In her left hand riches and honor.
"'Her ways *are* ways of pleasantness,
"'And all her paths are peace.'"

Don switched to a short excerpt from a classical piece to signify a transition in the service.

The minister stepped forward. "Hello, again," he said. "I am Pastor Wilbur Plain, and the minister of Pineville Community Church.

"I must say Elizabeth and Rick made this service verse I normally use for weddings, plus a few more."

The congregation smiled or laughed. A few adjusted themselves in their seats as though preparing for a long, continued sit.

"Actually, there are many more passages in the Bible that speak of marriage and love. I am extremely pleased that this couple, and many of the readers here today, took time in the Word to find Biblical messages for their earthly wishes. It speaks to their commitment to this couple and to God. This moved me as a minister more than you can imagine. It does happen, but not nearly as often as I would like."

The minister looked to a different section of the pews.

"In conjunction with Rick and Elizabeth's wishes for their ceremony, I want to focus on a few things that I think are particularly appropriate for this couple," he said.

"I have known both these young people all their lives,"

Pastor Plain continued. "I baptized Elizabeth. I confirmed both of them. Rick and Elizabeth had their first communion here, and my grandniece is Julia, who is now married to Elizabeth's brother, Lucas."

He looked down at his notes and then back at the congregation that filled the pews.

"So, here we are, on this beautiful autumn Saturday, celebrating a love that has been shared for years," the minister continued. "It has had its share of ups and downs, as many do. However, Rick and Elizabeth have made it through those trials, and they stand here before you today, ready to make a commitment to each other and to God."

He adjusted the microphone a bit.

"I have two more passages for you today. I will begin my wedding sermon with one and close the sermon with the other."

He looked out at the congregation.

"The first of my readings was actually the first reading the couple chose for this day, and it was Rick's selection."

Zietta Nerva smiled at her nephew.

"Please stand as I read from 1 Corinthians 13: verses 4 through the beginning of 8:

> "'Love suffers long *and* is kind; love does not envy; love does not parade itself, is not puffed up; does not behave rudely, does not seek its own, is not provoked, thinks no evil; does not rejoice in iniquity, but rejoices in the truth; bears all things, believes all things, hopes all things, endures all things.
>
> "'Love never fails.'"

The pastor spoke of the passage and of marital love. His message wasn't long, but it was supportive and beautiful.

He concluded with the words of 1 Corinthians 13:13:

"'And now abide faith, hope, love, these three; but the

greatest of these *is* love.'"

He closed his Bible and stepped to the middle of the altar.

"As we now move into the Unity Candle portion of this ceremony," said Pastor Plain, "Elizabeth has asked to do things a little differently. Customarily, it is only the bride and groom who come together to light this candle. That will not change, for it is their unity that we are celebrating today."

The minister nodded to Emmie and Charlie and the ushers to come forward. Each of them took a box of small white candles with drip rings at the bottom.

"As the flower girl and ring bearer, plus our ushers for this service come to you, they will be handing out candles to each person," said the minister. "After Rick and Elizabeth each bring their own candles to the center to signify their desire to be joined as one, their parents will come next. They will take their unlit candles and light them from the flame of the Unity Candle. This will signify their intent to support this couple in their marriage. Following the parents, will be the bridal party. Thereafter, each of you, beginning with those in the front of the church, will come forward to light yours. You also will be making a commitment to, and a prayer for, this couple."

The ceremony continued. As Elizabeth and Rick lit their own candles, the back-up organist began to play a gorgeous piece of emotion-filled music.

Once the candle ceremony was complete, the minister spoke directly to the couple.

"Elizabeth Jeannie Anderson, you have chosen a passage from Ruth to include in your vows. I ask you now to say those words to Rick."

Elizabeth said, "'Ruth 1: a portion of verse 16 and all of verse 17:

>"'Entreat me not to leave you,
>"'*Or to* turn back from following you;
>"'For wherever you go, I will go;

"'And wherever you lodge, I will lodge;
"'Your people *shall* be my people,
"'And your God, my God.
"'Where you die, I will die,
"'And there will I be buried.
"'The LORD do so to me, and more also,
"'If *anything* but death parts you and me.'"

The minister said, "Elizabeth, take Rick's hands in yours and repeat after me, I, Elizabeth Jeannie Anderson, take you, Ricardo Salvatore Polisari, Jr., to be my wedded husband, from this day forward. It is my desire to be with you through all that life unfolds."

Elizabeth repeated her vows.

"If this is truly your desire, I ask you to say, 'I do,'" said Pastor Plain.

"I do," said Elizabeth.

The minister turned his attention to Rick.

"Ricardo Salvatore Polisari, Jr., you have chosen a passage from the Song of Solomon to include in your vows. I ask you now to say those words to Elizabeth."

Rick cleared his throat and began. "'Song of Solomon, chapter 8, verses 6 through the beginning of 7:

"'Set me as a seal upon your heart,
"'As a seal upon your arm;
"'For love *is as* strong as death,
"'Jealousy *as* cruel as the grave;
"'Its flames *are* flames of fire,
"'A most vehement flame.
"'Many waters cannot quench love,
"'Nor can the floods drown it.'"

The minister said, "Rick, take Elizabeth's hands in yours and repeat after me, I, Ricardo Salvatore Polisari, Jr., take you, Elizabeth Jeannie Anderson, to be my wedded wife, from this day forward. It is my desire to be with you through all that life unfolds."

Rick repeated his vows.

"If this is truly your desire, I ask you to say, 'I do,'" said Pastor Plain.

"I do," said Rick.

"By the power vested in me by God, the Pineville Community Church and the state of Wisconsin, I now pronounce you husband and wife," said Pastor Plain.

He looked at Rick. "You may kiss your bride."

Rick lifted the lightly pearled veil from Elizabeth's face and put it backward over the main veil on the back of her head. He kissed her tenderly, then held her tightly.

"I conclude this service with the passage with which we began. It is the one that was read to you by Elizabeth's oldest brother, Joseph. It is Mark 10:9 which says:

> "'Therefore what God has joined together, let not man separate.'"

He put one hand over Rick's head and the other over Elizabeth's. "Ladies and gentlemen, Mr. and Mrs. Ricardo Polisari."

Chapter Thirty-Two

The couple made their way around the crowded room, greeting each and every guest. Dinner was over, and the band was setting up on the small stage at the front corner of the Pineville Diner and Campground Clubhouse. The walk through the room featured many stops that were not much more than a hello and a congratulations, but some were memorable beyond the cordialities.

"Betsy, you love my son," said Rick's dad.

"I do," said Elizabeth.

He pointed his finger at her. "You keep loving him. I know you wondered, but I tell you this as his father. He never stopped loving you. You honor that. He will honor you."

"Yes, sir," said Elizabeth. She gave him a hug and whispered in his ear. "Thank you."

When they reached Zietta Nerva's table, the woman eyed Elizabeth from top to bottom. "Now, you look like a bride should look," she said.

"Thank you, Zietta," said Elizabeth.

"You and Ricardo drive to see me this summer," she said. "I will show you the right way to make linguine with clam sauce."

Elizabeth stifled a laugh and gave her a big smile. "We will do that."

As they walked away, Rick said to her, "You'd better follow up with her after we get back from our honeymoon because if you don't actually go there, she won't forget that until the day she dies. She won't let you forget that, either."

"Gotcha," said Elizabeth.

When they reached the table with Stephanie's brother and parents, the couple sat for a moment.

"Thank you, both, for all the help with the move," said Johnny.

"Yes," said Tim, "there's no way Dad and I could have unloaded that in one afternoon by ourselves."

"Oh, now, Tim," said Barbara, "you're exaggerating!"

Tim gave his mother a knowing look. "I'm heading to the cake table," said Tim. "Roxanna, would you care to join me?"

"Absolutely," said Roxanna.

"You know," said Barbara. She kept her voice somewhat low as though conveying a secret. "Those two could be the next ones down the aisle."

When Elizabeth and Rick left that table to visit other guests, Rick said, "Are Tim and Roxanna a couple now?"

"Only in Barbara's imagination," said Elizabeth. "Tim and Roxanna have formed an alliance. Anytime either of them needs a 'plus one,' the other is there. They are both dedicatedly single. However, they talk all night and dance just enough for people to think they're together."

"I can't tell you how glad I am that you two finally got married," said Joseph as they found him at the clubhouse bar.

"We're pretty happy about it, too," said Rick. He leaned over and lightly kissed her on the lips.

"Rick said you had to leave church for some work thing," said Elizabeth. "Is everyone ok?"

Joseph took a sip from his beer and thought for a second before answering. "Not completely, but I think they will be."

They were most of the way through the room when the band announced the first song and asked that the bride and groom lead off the dancing.

Rick and Elizabeth began their first dance as husband and wife. Elizabeth's eyes were closed, and she rested her head on his chest.

As other couples joined the floor, Rick said, "Oh, no."

Elizabeth opened her eyes and looked at him. "What is it?"

Rick nodded towards the back of the dance floor. "Michael is dancing with Trish."

"I hope that doesn't hurt Melissa's feelings," said Elizabeth. "I have a feeling that my brother will dance with lots of women tonight."

"I know Trisha," said Rick. "She'll wrap him right around her finger, which is exactly where she prefers men should be.

"Michael's not looking for a girlfriend," said Elizabeth.

"Maybe not," said Rick, "but if Trisha has her way, he won't be dancing with anyone else tonight."

"She's not going to have her way," said Elizabeth.

"What makes you think that?" asked Rick.

"Because during the bridal party dance, he needs to dance with Melissa," said Elizabeth.

At one point during the evening, Rick and Michael were at the punchbowl at the same time.

"Be careful," said Rick.

"Why?" asked Michael.

Rick looked toward Trisha. "High maintenance," he said.

Michael grabbed two punch cups. "Don't care," he replied.

Rick found his way back to Elizabeth and gave her a cup of punch. "It's already happened," he said. "Trisha has roped in your brother."

Elizabeth looked at the table where Michael was now hanging on every word Rick's cousin, Trisha, said.

"Ah," said Elizabeth. She pulled Rick over to the stage with her. She spoke to the sound guy for the band. "Could you play the bridal party dance now?" she asked.

The sound guy nodded. "Next up?" he asked.

"Perfect," said Elizabeth.

As the song ended, the sound guy called the lead singer over to the side.

"Ladies and gentlemen," the singer said into his microphone. "It is time for our bridal party dance! I'd like to introduce each person or couple and ask that they come out to the dance floor at that time."

He looked at some notes he had jotted in his cell phone. "First of all, our littlest members, the mini ring bearer and flower girls, Margaret, Jackson, and Jillian Anderson!"

There was a round of applause as Julia and Stephanie and brought their toddlers out onto the dance floor.

"Uh, they won't be dancing with us tonight, but they sure are adorable, aren't they?" said the singer.

"Next up, our Flower Girl and Ring Bearer, Emmie and Charlie Anderson!" the singer announced.

Emmie and Charlie came on the floor with the assistance of Angela who had corralled them into place.

"Our next couple is Bridesmaid, Melissa Polisari and Groomsman, Michael Anderson!"

Michael and Melissa came onto the floor amidst cheers and applause. Being the only Polisari in the actual bridal party itself, there was much hooting and hollering of applause from Rick's side of the family. Rick noted that Trisha was pouting at the table, having been left alone for Michael to fulfill duties as one of the wedding party.

"Now, please welcome Bridesmaid, Bridget O'Dunn and Groomsman, Lucas Anderson!"

Lucas and Bridget came out onto the dance floor as Julia smiled while Margaret strained in Julia's arms to reach her daddy.

"Here comes your Maid of Honor and Best Man, Angela Anderson and Joseph Anderson!" announced the singer.

Angela and Joseph joined the group on the dance floor.

"Please put your hands together for our bride and groom, Elizabeth and Rick!" the singer called out with enthusiasm.

Rick and Elizabeth once more came onto the dance floor.

The party continued for a couple more hours. As the evening slowed, and a number of the guests departed, Rick and Elizabeth found some time to talk with Eugene.

"Geno," said Rick, "I guess I really do need to thank you."

"You know I'm always happy to take pictures," said Eugene.

"That, too," said Rick.

"Too?" said Eugene. "Oh, yes, well, you know I also love playing the accordion, and I had extra fun teaming up with Elizabeth's dad for a couple of numbers."

Rick shook his head and looked at him.

"The tap dancing?" said Eugene. "You know, I enjoy that, but I mainly do it to get on Zietta Nerva's nerves."

Rick shook his head no.

"Well, there's nothing else for which to thank me," said Eugene. "So, let's not discuss."

"No," said Rick, "I will discuss it. If you don't want to answer me, obviously you don't have to do so. However, I need to say this, and I need you to hear it."

"All right," said Eugene. "Unnecessary, but all right."

"Look," said Rick, "I'm not quite sure how you figured all that stuff with Randy and Elizabeth and myself out, but I do know this. I never really fathomed that was at the bottom of it, or at least a part of the bottom."

"I was right," said Eugene.

"Yes, you were," said Rick.

"That's not what I meant," said Eugene.

"Then what do you mean?" asked Rick.

"That it's totally unnecessary to discuss," said Eugene. "However, I have something that I want to say to you, too."

"What's that?" asked Rick.

"This has been a wonderful wedding," said Eugene. "I was thrilled to be asked to be a part of it. You picked a great time of year, too. The changing colors of the leaves, just a hint of cool in the air. It was ideal. I've been to other fall weddings, but it never seemed like the season was part and parcel of the day, only a sidebar. I like when things are all tied together. I think that's why I like photography so much. You can capture so much that otherwise fades out of memory within a short time."

"Well," said Rick, "now you know. If you ever get married, you can have it here at this time of year."

Eugene tilted his head at Rick. "That's unlikely to be anytime soon. However, I will file that away in my own memory." He pretended to write on a sheet of paper. "For a perfect day, have a Pineville autumn wedding."

Cast of Characters

"A Pineville Autumn Wedding"

In alphabetical order

Angela Anderson	Youngest daughter of Don and Jeannie, works at the Pineville Diner and Campground
Arthur Hodges	Myrtle's late husband, father of Susan
Barbara Cannady	Stephanie's mother, Johnny's wife, grandmother of Emmie, Charlie, Jackson, and Jillian Anderson
Bonnie Jorgenson	Sister of Jeannie Anderson, owner of the Main Street Bakery in Pineville
Bridget O'Dunn	Elizabeth's veterinary assistant and friend
Carlo Polisari	Rick's uncle and Nerva's brother
Charlie Anderson	Six-year-old son of Joseph and Stephanie Anderson
Chiara Travesti	Rick's cousin, daughter of Nerva

Chloe	Teenager at the Milwaukee airport travelling with her parents
Deke Anderson	Married to Myrtle, Don's brother and uncle to the Anderson family, co-owner of the Pineville Diner and Campground
Don Anderson	Married to Jeannie, father of the Anderson family, co-owner of the Pineville Diner and Campground, and church organist at the Pineville Community Church
Elizabeth Anderson	Don and Jeannie's oldest daughter, fiancé of Rick Polisari, veterinarian, and owner of Yarkton House
Emmie Anderson	Eight-year-old daughter of Joseph and Stephanie Anderson
Eugene Winebush	Rick's cousin
Jackson Anderson	Infant son of Joseph and Stephanie
Jeannie Anderson	Mother of the Anderson family, Don's wife, and co-owner of the Pineville Diner and Campground
Jillian Anderson	Infant daughter of Joseph and Stephanie
Johnny Cannady	Father of Stephanie, married to Barbara, grandfather of Emmie, Charlie, Jackson, and Jillian Anderson

Joseph Anderson	Oldest son in the Anderson family, husband of Stephanie, father of Emmie, Charlie, Jackson, and Jillian, town sheriff
Julia Anderson	Wife of Lucas Anderson, mother of Margaret, and secretary of the Pineville Community Church
Lucas Anderson	Second oldest son in the Anderson family, husband of Julia, father of Margaret, high school history teacher, and summer worker at the campground
Margaret Anderson	Infant daughter of Lucas and Julia
Melissa Polisari	Rick's cousin
Michael Anderson	Fourth child in Don and Jeannie's family, works odd jobs and at the campground
Myrtle Anderson	Former church secretary at the Pineville Community Church, Julia's predecessor, married to Deke, mother of Susan
Nerva Polisari-Travesti	Rick's aunt
Pastor Wilbur Plain	Julia's granduncle, and minister of Pineville Community Church
Randy Numetz	Elizabeth's former boyfriend

Rick Polisari	Owner of Rick's Pizza, friend of the Anderson brothers, Elizabeth's fiancé
Roxanna Cartos	Local artist and part-time waitress at the Pineville Diner and Rick's Pizza
Sniffy	Elizabeth's allergy-ridden dog
Stephanie Anderson	Wife of Joseph Anderson, mom to Emmie, Charlie, Jackson, and Jillian, best friend of Julia, and kindergarten teacher
Susan Hodges	Myrtle's daughter
Tim Cannady	Stephanie's brother, son of Johnny and Barbara
Tracy Anderson	Joseph's late wife and mother of Emmie and Charlie
Trisha Polisari	Rick's cousin
Vicky Walker	Former friend of Rick and Elizabeth's

Coming Soon

From the Pineville Series...

A Pineville Christmas Past
Anticipated release November 2022

From the When Life Changes Series...

Wasted In Milwaukee
Anticipated release date summer, 2023

&

From the Writings of My Faith Series...

Apologies, Forgiveness, & Acceptance
Anticipated release date January,2024

All titles and dates are subject to change.

<h1 style="text-align:center">About the Author</h1>

Anne Fons lives with her husband and mother in Wisconsin. She is the mom of four adult children and grandma to one grandson and numerous grand pets.

During her work career, she held several positions including that of a radio newsperson and an IT customer service manager.

She describes herself as a 'full-life' advocate. She encourages people to live life to its fullest regardless of age. She encourages seniors to make the latter half of their lives as fulfilling as the first.

For signing or speaking engagements, write:
Appearance
Anne Fons Readers Group
P.O. Box 620044
Middleton, WI 53562